THE BEAST BETWEEN MY SHEETS 2

J'DIORR

D1518190

The Beast Between My Sheets 2
Copyright 2019 by J'Diorr

Published by Mz. Lady P Presents

Previously...

A'miracle

Sitting in Northwestern Hospital, I was praying harder than I've ever prayed in my life. I didn't know what condition my father was in, but I begged God not to take my Superman away from me. I needed my father more than anything. I wondered was it something I said? Was it anything I've could have done? No one wants to wake up to one of their parents on the floor. He was so cold, but he was sweating too, which was odd. I called out to him what felt like a million times, and he didn't answer, or look my way. My mom was devastated, but I knew she was trying to be strong for me. My hands were shaking so badly that I couldn't focus.

"A'miracle, it's going to be ok. I worship an awesome God, and He will not forsake us, my dear," my mother said, with tears in her eyes. I just simply laid my head on her shoulder and continued to pray. It felt like we waited in the waiting area for hours before the nurse finally called my mother's name. Quickly, we both got up and followed her.

We were taken to the Nephrology floor of the hospital, and I was a bit confused. I thought maybe my father had fallen, suffered a stroke, or was having a heart attack, not this. Looking around, I knew my mother sensed I was nervous about everything, but she kept reassuring me that everything would be fine. We made it to my father's room, and the nurse said the doctor would be in shortly. Once I laid eyes on him, I ran over to the bed so fast, and wrapped my arms around my father. Again, I cried so hard, knowing something was wrong with him. I felt his hand rub my back before he removed the mask that was covering his mouth.

"It's ok, baby girl. Your old man will be fine," my father said, coughing.

"No, Daddy, keep that on, and don't talk. Get your rest," I said, kissing his cheek before wiping my face. My mother walked to the opposite side of the bed and kissed my father, before pulling the chair in the corner closest to him.

"You scared me," she said, fighting back tears, and I watched as my father reassured her that everything would be fine. I was on pins and needles, waiting for the doctor to come and tell me what was wrong with my father. All of the information on the board in front of us made no sense. I didn't know what any of this stuff meant. I just knew my father was in the hospital, and things weren't good. My phone vibrated in my hands, and it was a message from Tabari. As bad as I wanted to reply, I chose not to, since my mind was on my father. I just needed him to get better.

"A'miracle, come here," my father called out to me, and I rushed to his side. I could see the tears emerging in his eyes, and I knew this had to be bad.

"Listen to me, no matter what the doctor's say, I'm going to be ok. Don't you worry about a thing. I love you so much, princess," my father said, just as the doctor walked in.

"Hello, I'm Dr. Kirby. I'm a Nephrologist. Can you state your name and date of birth for me, sir? Gotta make sure I have the right file," Dr. Kirby asked, looking down at the folder he was holding.

"Nephrologist?" I asked, confused, looking over at my mother. She placed her hand up, basically telling me to calm down and wait, but I couldn't.

"My name is Harrison Evans. Date of birth is 8/10/1967," my father replied, placing the mask back over his face.

"Ok, Mr. Evans, how are you feeling? Any pain?" He asked, walking over to my father.

"Yea, a little," my dad said.

"Where is it? And how would you rate the pain? Zero being none, and ten being the worse pain you've ever felt," Dr. Kirby asked, squeezing hand sanitizer on his hands before lifting the cover off my father.

"I think my pain is around a seven," my father stated, looking over at me. I prayed nothing was seriously wrong. I can't lose my father.

"Does it hurt when I push here?" Dr. Kirby asked, pressing down on the lower parts of my father's stomach. With each push, my father said yes, and it literally, broke my heart to see him in pain like this.

"Ok, Mr. Evans. I'm going to get you some pain meds, and start a morphine drip. That should help manage the pain for now. Also, as I told you, your kidneys are failing, and you need a transplant. I've already placed you on the list. Do you understand?" Dr. Kirby asked, but I didn't.

"Wait, Daddy, you need a kidney?" I asked, grabbing the wall to keep me from falling.

"I'm fine, baby girl," my father said, but I didn't believe him.

"So, Dr. Kirby, how does this work? What happens if he gets a kidney?" I asked, looking directly at him.

"I'm sorry, ma'am, you are?"

"His daughter, A'miracle. Now, please answer my question. What happens to my father?" I asked, more firmly.

"Well, Ms. A'miracle, your father is very sick. I understand that he was a firefighter, and now chief. His job may have been the cause of this, but once we run more tests we will see. Right now, your father is going to go on dialysis as well. We have to clean all the toxins out of his blood, since his kidneys aren't working properly. Right now, no need to panic. Your father is in good care, and I will do my best, A'miracle," Dr. Kirby stated.

"So, we're basically waiting for someone to die to give him a kidney?" I asked, causing my mother to gasp.

"A'miracle?"

"No, Ma, I'm just trying to get a clearer understanding. I didn't mean for it to come out that way. You know I would never disrespect anyone. My apologies, doctor," I said, looking at him.

"No, no, that's what I'm here for. To answer these types of questions. So, no, we aren't waiting for someone to die to get a kidney. We're simply waiting for a kidney that matches his blood type. That person could be deceased, or very much alive. We have two kidneys, and you can actually live a full life with one. So, we're just waiting for a donor," Dr. Kirby stated. Looking over at my father, I knew I couldn't let him die. I knew what the doctor told me, but I also watch a lot of Grey's Anatomy. If my father didn't get a kidney soon, things would get worse. I couldn't sit back and watch my father deteriorate. I would never forgive myself if I did.

"Ok, well, where do I sign up?"

"A'miracle! No! You will not do this," my father stated, but I ignored him.

"Where do I sign up, Dr. Kirby? Test me, and see if I match. He's my father, so I should be," I expressed.

"A'miracle, please just listen to your-"

"No, Ma! I can't sit around and hope for something like this. Do you know how many people are on the transplant list? Why wait around for one and I have two? Dr. Kirby said that you can live a perfect life with one kidney, and if that's the case, and I'm a match, then I'm giving my father one! I can't sit back and watch him die, Mama, I can't," I cried, looking at her. She looked over at my father, and I didn't know what they said with their eyes, but it wasn't good. I brushed it off and followed the doctor out of the room.

"This is Nurse Jill, and she will take you to the lab for blood work. We have to make sure you're a match. I have a few questions though," Dr. Kirby said, but I already knew what he was going to ask.

"I'm 26 years old, born December 25, 1992. I don't have any children. Never been pregnant. No history of STD's. I don't smoke or drink. My health is absolutely perfect, and I'm a donor," I said, assuring him as he nodded his head.

"Well, I'll be the judge of your health, as soon as we get this blood work back, A'miracle. I really think this is a lovely thing you're doing for your father. God bless you," Dr. Kirby said to me, as I followed the nurse to the lab. Once inside, I had to sign some paperwork before they gave me a patient wristband. The entire time I was nervous and prayed that everything came back normal. I didn't wanna lose my father, and I would kill and bring him a kidney if I had to. The nurse took about three tubes of blood before walking me back to the room. My father was fast asleep, and my mother had tears in her eyes.

"A'miracle, are you absolutely sure?" My mother asked.

"Yes, Mama, I am. If I'm a match, I'm giving Daddy a kidney. It's ok, I'm ok, and we will get through this," I said, trying to reassure her now.

"I know, but, never mind," my mother said, shaking her head as she held my father's hand. For the remainder of the time, we didn't say anything, and before I knew it, we both dozed off. I woke up to the sound of voices outside of the room. I looked over at my parents, and they both were sleeping. Hearing Dr. Kirby's mouth, I walked over to the door to listen. I could hear them clearly, but what they were saying wasn't making sense.

"Yes, Dr. Kirby. The blood types don't match, but the crazy thing is that the mother's blood type was saved in the system. She came in for tests months ago. Comparing all three, there is no way the mom's blood type, and father's blood type could create A negative," Nurse Jill stated. I watched as Dr. Kirby went over the paperwork in his hands and waited for him to speak. But what he said next I wasn't expecting.

"So, he's not her father? Well, they're not her parents," he said, shaking his head, and the moment that left his lips, I gasped and opened the door.

"What did you just say?" I asked, and watched as Dr. Kirby's face turned pale.

"Ms. Evans, umm, go back inside. I'll be in in a second to check on your father," Dr. Kirby said, but I knew what I heard him say, and there was no way in hell I was going back inside.

"Dr. Kirby, I heard you say that they're not my parents. Isn't that what you said?" I asked, but instead of replying, he simply said he was sorry, and quickly walked away. I walked back into the room and turned the light on. As soon as I did, my mother looked up at me, before looking over at my father.

"Did the doctor's come back? What did they say about your test?" My mother asked, or shall I say, this woman.

"The test came back, and I'm not a match," I said, looking at her.

"Oh, sweetie, I'm so sorry, but God-"

"They said I'm not a match, and your two blood types together wouldn't make mine. So, you're not my parents?" I stated, but more of a question than a statement. My mother's eyes got big, and I knew right then and there it was true.

"So, you've been lying to me my entire life?" I asked, looking at the tears well up in her eyes.

"A'miracle, let me explain," she asked, but I shook my head no.

"Explain what? I'm not your daughter. At 26 years old, I find out that my entire life was a lie, and I don't even know who the fuck my parents are," I said, cursing, which was something I've never done in front of my mother.

"A'miracle, please," she begged.

"No, I can't do this right now," I said, grabbing my purse and car keys. I quickly left the room and ran out of the hospital. As soon as I got to my car, I couldn't breathe. It felt like the wind was knocked out of me, and the scream I allowed to escape my lungs was one from the pits of my soul. I cried so hard for about twenty minutes before I finally calmed myself. I didn't know what to do, or who to call.

My phone rang, and it was my mother, or the woman who portrayed to be my mother, and I quickly ignored her call. Not only did I get my ass whooped days ago, but I was also raped by a man I loved, and possibly wanted to spend the rest of my life with. Then, I reconnected with my father, who almost died in the kitchen. Only to get to the hospital to find out he needed a kidney, and to take the test to find out I'm not a match. But the icing on the cake was the fact that my blood type was so different, that it didn't match theirs, which means I'm not their child. Who the fuck goes through shit like this? This sounds like something in a movie, or in a fucking book! I needed to get away, I had to get away from here. Pulling out of the parking lot, I called Tabari.

"Hey, beautiful, how are you?" He asked, but I was crying too bad to answer him.

"Baby, what's wrong?" He asked, causing me to break down even more. I just kept shaking my head, until I got my thoughts together.

"Talk to me, sweetie, where are you?" Tabari asked, with so much concern.

"Please, I need you. Send me your location, so I can come to you," I cried. Moments later, my phone beeped.

"I'm on my way," I said, but he didn't let me end the call. He literally, told me that I didn't have to say anything until I got to him. He wanted to stay on the phone to make sure I was safe. This man was so damn sweet, and it's crazy how I continue to run to him for comfort. Tabari was everything I wanted Wade to be. He was caring, goal oriented, fine as hell, and put me first.

"How far are you?" Tabari asked.

"I just pulled up in front of my house. I need to grab something really quickly, and I will be to you. GPS says I'm only twelve minutes away," I said, getting out of the car. I walked inside my condo and locked the door behind me. I turned on the light and screamed, dropping my phone.

"Who the fuck are you? How did you get in here?" I asked the man sitting on my couch, holding one of the biggest knives I've ever laid eyes on. I could hear Tabari calling me, but I was too afraid to pick up the phone.

"A'miracle, I'm Lazer. Sorry to meet you like this, sweetie, and I had to ruin your day," he smirked, which caused chills all over.

"Why don't you have a seat, so we can chat a little?" Lazer

stated. I looked over at him and to the door wondering if I should make a run for it.

"Don't try to run either, child, it would only piss me off more. Have a seat, dear, I won't ask again," Lazer stated. I could feel the tears forming in my eyes, as I picked up my phone and sat on the couch. I could hear Tabari yelling my name, but I was too afraid to answer. I knew whatever this man was here for had something to do with Wade. I wasn't up for any more bad news. I wasn't sure if I could take it.

"Your boyfriend, Wade, owes me a lot of money, and he told me specifically, I could get it from you," he smirked, licking his lips. At the sight of him, my skin crawled, I was so damn scared, that I was shaking.

"No tears, dear, I only want one thing, we can make this easy, or take the hard road. The choice is yours. Now, where is your room?" He asked, standing, and I already knew what that meant, and what was about to occur. I got up and walked away, and he followed closely behind me. Once inside my room, I finally answered Tabari.

"I gotta call you back," I whispered, not even waiting for him to reply before I ended the call. I watched as this man looked at me, and I wanted to die exactly where I stood. A part of me did die, Rest In Peace to me…

ONE

A'miracle

W here we left off...

"Agh," I screamed out, as I was roughly thrown on the bed. Trying to fight back, Lazer pinned me down using his weight, and pulled my hands above my head.

"If you scream, or do anything stupid, I will cut your body open and watch you bleed out," Lazer stated, causing me not to move.

"Now, my dear," he said, as he used the machete to roam my body. It literally, went from my neck, down to my chest; from my chest, down to my stomach, and when he made it to my private area, he stopped and looked at me. By now, the tears were flowing, and I just wanted this to be over.

"Wade owes me a lot of money. I told him already that if he didn't pay up, or tried some funny shit, I would kill you," he stated, in a voice that made my skin crawl. I don't know if I was more upset that he told Wade he would kill me, or the fact his ass didn't attempt to stop him.

"You see, I'm not that bad; actually, I am, but you're cute, and I think you deserve a chance. I know there's no money here, because I've already looked. I'm giving you, let's say, two weeks, to come up with the money. If you don't have it, A'miracle, then that's really

1

going to piss me off and a bunch of other big scary men. They won't be as nice as I am to you, and I promise, you don't want that. By the time they finished with you, you'll be begging for them to kill you. Now, I'm sure you know how this goes, since you fuck with a street nigga. The police can't save you, and if you contact them in any way, I will kill your mother. Then I will probably fuck your father up enough where he doesn't die, but he wishes he had. You don't wanna be on my bad side, because your boyfriend already is. Contact him the best way you can, and he will tell you how much is owed; plus, interest. You look like a smart girl. Probably came from rich parents, so I'm sure you can get the money from somewhere. Don't you wanna save your boyfriend's life? Do it for love; you know, that whole ride or die thing. I'll be in touch," Lazer said, walking out of my room. I heard the front door close before I got up and got my phone.

My hands were shaking.

My pulse was racing.

I was so damn scared, that I couldn't even unlock my phone to call Tabari back. When I did, he answered on the first ring.

"A'miracle? Are you ok?" He asked, as I heard what sounded like the car door opening.

"No! This man had a knife. He threatened me. He told me he will kill me and my family if I don't pay him money and-"

Before I had a chance to explain, there was a knock at the door.

"That's me, open the door," Tabari said, and I raced to the door. The moment I opened it, I fell into his arms and cried so damn hard. I couldn't believe all this shit was happening to me. This doesn't happen to girls like me. I don't do shit to anyone, so why is it that folks wanna harm and hurt A'miracle? All I wanted was a nice, normal life, and now that was out of the question. Because of my actions, and involvement with a nigga, now I was in hot water for some shit he's done. And the fucked-up part about it is I'm positive Wade doesn't give a damn. I'm sure his ass is miles away, saving himself!

I couldn't be mad at anyone but me. I should have been left his ass alone a long time ago, but here I was, holding on to memories. I was holding on to moments that we shared. I was holding on to the place when we were genuinely happy. I was holding on to a love that was broken, but I constantly hurt myself trying to put the pieces back together. This was what a fool does. A dumb ass fool in love.

"Are you ok? Did he hurt you?" Tabari asked, letting me go and looking over me.

"You're bleeding. Here sit down," he said, as he walked me over to the couch. The moment he said that, I touched my neck, and my hand did have blood on it.

"He didn't cut you anywhere else, did he?" Tabari asked, placing a cool towel on my neck. I was in so much shock, that I didn't even know I was bleeding.

"No, I don't think so," I said, staring off into space.

"It's not deep at all, and it should stop bleeding in a few minutes. Come on, you're coming with me. We're going back to my place. You're not safe here anymore," Tabari said, helping me up.

"Wait, but what about my stuff, and-"

"A'miracle, your life is more important than this material shit. I will purchase everything you need, but right now, we need to leave," Tabari said, pulling out a gun. I watched as he ejected a magazine before clicking it back in and pulling one in the chamber. He placed it back on his side, and guided me to the door. Once we were outside, he guided me to his car. He made sure I was strapped in before going over to the driver's side and speeding off.

"A'miracle, listen to me, and listen to me good. Wade is foul. That nigga has fucked over so many people, and he has a lot of people in fucked up situations because of his actions. That nigga that was at your house today, when I find him, I'm going to kill him. Not only is he responsible for the death of my uncle, but he tried to harm you. Wade, when I catch that motherfucker, I'm going to kill him as well, because he set my uncle up," Tabari stated, confusing the fuck out of me.

"Wait, what? He set who up? Wade wouldn't do-"

"Please don't defend that nigga in my car, A'miracle," Tabari said, looking over at me. I could tell he was pissed off and I've never seen him mad before. I felt stupid saying that shit. Just look at my predicament. It was a whole nigga with a big ass machete sitting in my house, waiting for me, and my dumbass was defending the nigga responsible.

"I'm sorry. I didn't mean it like that," I said, barely above a whisper.

"I know you didn't. I also know this is a lot to take in right now. But I need you to know that you can trust me, and I will protect you, A'miracle. I need you to stay the fuck away from Wade. No contact at all, because I don't want you to get hurt. Do you understand?" Tabari asked, and I looked over at him. I couldn't help but admire him. Here he is ready to protect me, and he barely even knows me. Whereas, my boyfriend of all these years literally, left my ass for the wolves. Guess his personality really does match his alter ego. Wolfe, who the fuck thinks of that?

"I understand. Your uncle who got killed, was his name C-Mack?" I asked.

"Yea, that's him," Tabari stated, not even looking over at me. I simply placed my hand on top of his and held it. I couldn't believe the things I was hearing. Wade cried really hard about the death of C-Mack, and come to find out, his ass is responsible. I couldn't believe I was sleeping next to someone like this. How could he do something like this?

"I'm sorry about your uncle, Tabari. I really am," I said, hoping to make him feel better.

"And I'm sorry that you have to experience this shit. The only reason I told you was because I wanted you to know everything. There's no denying something is here, A'miracle, and like I told you, I'm not rushing you or nothing, but a nigga feeling you. I'm going to do everything in my power to protect you and make this nightmare we both are living in disappear. I just need you to trust me and my judgment. You may not always agree with the shit I'm going to tell you, ask of you, or just shit that I can't explain. I just need you to listen to me, and know I will never put you in harm's way," Tabari said, making a right turn. The block was filled with a lot of nice-looking houses. Crazy how I lived in Chicago all my life, and never even knew a block like this existed, especially on the west side of Chicago.

"I want you to stay with me for a while, A'miracle. There is more than enough space here for you. And before you get to thinking, I'll tell you. No, I don't have any kids, or baby mama drama. I don't really fuck with people, so only a few know where I lay my head at. I take care of my mother and my baby sister, so if either of them ever calls for anything, it's a must that I go and see what's going on. So, don't think I'm ignoring you or anything like that. That's not the case. They are literally, all I have. As for my relationship, I'm single. Yes, I entertain, or have entertained, a few women here and there, but nothing is serious. I'm just putting everything out on the table, so you can get to know the real me. I'm letting you know up front what it is, what it ain't, and what it's going to be. It's up to you, in the end, to figure out if you wanna fuck with a nigga or not," Tabari said, getting out of the car. He walked over to my door and opened it. I unbuckled my seatbelt, grabbed his hand, and got out of the car.

"Don't worry about your car. Either I'll have one of my boys go pick it up for you, or put you in a rental. I know you have to work and handle things with your family," Tabari said, causing me to sigh heavily. Just thinking about my business burning to the ground, and the fact that I don't even know who the hell I am anymore, was really taking a toll on me.

"Did I say something wrong?" Tabari asked, as he guided me to his front door. From the outside looking in the building looked like a two flat, but once I walked inside, I couldn't believe it. There were cherry hardwood floors throughout. What I assumed to be a two flat, was actually a two leveled home. The living room was huge, and the floor to ceiling windows were beautiful. I followed Tabari to the back, where we went down three tiny steps, and I was now in the dining room. The glass chandelier was pretty, above a six-foot, six-seater table. All the walls were off white, with paintings all around.

"I'm sorry if it's a mess in here. I'll clean up everything up for you. Let me take your coat," Tabari said, as I unbuttoned it, and handed it to him. He hung it up in the closet, then we made our way to the kitchen. The kitchen was just as big as the living room, with a bar directly in the middle of the floor. All of his appliances were silver, and I absolutely couldn't wait to cook in this kitchen. My God, there was a double oven separate from the enormous stove he had. I took a seat at the bar and took everything in around me.

"I can give you a tour, if you want?" Tabari said, smiling. I guess he caught on to the amazement I was feeling. This is a house that I would have loved to own. I would have loved to raise a family here.

"Yea, you can, but not right now. Mind if I have a drink? I have a lot on my mind," I said, putting my phone down. My mother had been calling me nonstop, and I refused to call her back. I was so angry inside, and I didn't know how to handle everything. It just felt like everything was happening too fast, too soon, and all at once. How can I get passed this shit?

"Yea, what's your favorite drink?" Tabari asked, washing his hands then going over to the bar.

"Right now, I need something hard. Fuck that fruity shit," I spat, shaking my head, and placing my arms on the table. I looked up at him as he laughed before grabbing two glasses.

"Ok, no fruity shit as you say. And what happened to your arm?" Tabari asked, reaching over and touching it.

"It's a birthmark. Well, that's what I was told. Now, I'm not sure if that's even true," I explained. Honestly, I didn't know. It looked like a huge keloid on my left forearm, as if I was burned by something.

"So, what are we drinking? Dark or light?" Tabari asked, licking his lips. I wanted to tell him I liked my men just like I liked my liquor, but I didn't wanna come off as a thot.

"We can do dark," I said, as he opened the refrigerator and pulled out a bottle of Hennessey. He pulled out a bottle of apple-cranberry juice and looked at me.

"What was that look for?" I smirked.

"Just in case you not a straight drinker. I can mix it up real good for you, and it'll taste just like juice," he offered, but I didn't want any juice right now. I needed something hard to calm my nerves.

"Nah, give me two pieces of ice, and pour that shit up," I said, sounding like the environment I grew up in.

"Yea, ok, we can go your way. But let me know when you want some juice," he said, in his Kevin Hart voice. We both busted into laughter as he moved the cups out of the way and filled two shot glasses.

"I feel like you need a few of these. Let's start here," Tabari said, placing a shot in front of me. Without thinking, I picked it up and tossed it back, before siding it over to him for a refill. I think my mind was so fucked up, that I ignored the burning sensation I felt. Instead, I welcomed it, hoping the intoxication level I would receive was better than the pain I was feeling. I knew the answer to my problems wasn't in the bottom of this bottle, but relaxation was, my peace was, and so was my sanity.

"Yea, my kind of drinker," he joked, filling my shot glass again. I tossed it back and he did the same before pouring himself another one. After the third round of shots, he poured us both a glass and sat next to me.

"Wanna talk about what happened earlier? I mean, not what just occurred, but when you called me crying? Things didn't go right with your parents?" He asked, in the most calming voice. His voice was so soothing, and he cared. He was nothing like Wade, who would have told me to suck that shit up and stop being weak. It's crazy how you start to see someone's true colors when you're on the outside looking in. I just shook my head before telling Tabari every-thing. I explained it from the beginning to the end, as well as showing him the missed calls I had from my mother. This was just too much right now, and I needed a vacation, even if I didn't physi-cally go anywhere. I'll let the drinks take my mind away.

"Damn, I'm sorry to hear that. I'm sorry you had to find out like this. I mean, damn," he said, shaking his head, causing me to laugh.

"That's all you have to say is damn?" I asked, shoving him.

"Nah, I don't mean it like that, A'miracle. I mean like, you just found out they're not your parents; not from their mouths, but from the doctors. What if the doctors got it wrong?" He asked, looking over at me. I didn't think about that. I literally, knew what I heard, and what the doctors said and ran with it.

"I mean, what if they messed up something? Mistakes happen all the time, A'miracle, especially in hospitals. I don't think this was something your parents would purposely keep from you. That's a big secret to keep. Don't you look like your parents?" He asked, causing me to look at him again. I never really paid attention to that. Quickly, I picked up my phone and showed him pictures of both my father and mother, but it wasn't anything significantly off. We all shared dark skin, so maybe he was right.

"Don't feed too much into it. I think it could be a big misunder-standing," Tabari said, giving me an ounce of hope. But realizing my mother did try to explain before I left, made me feel even worse. Maybe I should have stayed and heard her out. What if the things she was trying to tell me was something I needed to hear?

"Then, on top of everything, this motherfucker burned your establishment down? Damn, that's some cold-hearted shit," Tabari stated, shaking his head. I could see his jawline clenching, and I knew he was becoming upset. I think I was still in shock too. So much was happening, that I forgot to call the insurance company. That would be something I would handle tomorrow morning.

"Well, if it makes you feel any better, I can show you some of my work in person," he said, smirking.

"Like a building you made? That would be dope," I said, looking at him.

"Good, cause you're sitting in one," he said, causing my face to light up.

"Wait, you built this house?" I asked, excitedly.

"Yep, I built it for another contractor. He was trying to surprise his wife, but she ended up surprising him, by sleeping with his brother. Long story short, he gave it to me. Told me it was a token of his appreciation of my hard work. Been living here ever since," he said, honestly.

"Dang, that's crazy as hell, but a good thing for you," I said.

"Yea, it is, but when you living in this big ass house, with no one to share it with, it gets a lil lonely, you feel me?" He said, looking at me.

"Well, I'm here now, so you won't be lonely anymore," I said, more of the liquor talking than me. The more sips I took, the more relaxed I became.

"Come on, let me show you upstairs. You can pick out which room you wanna sleep in too," he stated.

"But I wanna sleep with you," I whispered.

"What you say?" Tabari asked.

"Nothing," I quickly said, laughing to myself, and following him upstairs.

TWO

Tabari

⸻

We damn near finished the whole fifth of Hennessey, while I showed A'miracle around my home. My place was indeed big, but lonely as hell, honestly. I had all these rooms that were empty, and no one to occupy them. So, you can imagine how I felt inside, having A'miracle here with me. She was going through a lot, and my heart went out to her. It's fucked up she had to find out about her parents the way that she did. It's even more fucked up that Wade's bitch ass burned her business down. I don't know what it was about this woman that had me willing to risk everything to help her, but I was willing to do it.

I couldn't lie, I wanted A'miracle bad. Not just on a sexual level, but a spiritual one. I wanted to fuck her mind first, make love to her soul entirely. Make her have multiple orgasms, without ever placing one finger on her. I wanted to open her mind up to endless possibilities, but I knew in order for me to have her, in order for me to have all of her, Wade's ass had to disappear. She can sit here and tell me she's over him, and she's never going back, but that would be bullshit. I know personally how hard it is to walk away from someone you love, even if they mean you no good.

Women tend to think that if they give it time, continue to put up with the bullshit, a man would change for them. Truth is, no woman, or amount of pussy, can change a man. A man changes because he wants to change. Women hold on to shit that's broken, because they've invested so much time, invested so much energy, into broken situations that they could never get back. Situations they should have left a long time ago, they continue to cut themselves, attempting to piece things back together. In the end, they're never truly happy with the ending results, because all of their happiness had already been depleted from their hearts.

They never truly love, because the love had already been sucked out from their pores, literally, leaving a mass of tissue in the form of a heart. So many women are in relationships just to be in one, because of the time they've invested. So many women are heartless now because of the nigga they chose to give their hearts to, which fucks up things for us good men. Looking at A'miracle, she was more relaxed now that the liquor was kicking in. The pain was still evident on her face, but she was still smiling. Honestly, I just wanted to make the damn girl feel better, and help her realize all men aren't the same.

"Where's your room?" A'miracle asked, breaking me from my thoughts. I didn't know if this was the alcohol talking, or if she was just curious. Shaking the thoughts from my head, I led her back down the hall and to my room. Once inside, she looked around before sitting on the bed. I knew she was drunk since her eyes were low, but she looked even more appealing. I couldn't keep my eyes off the damn girl. Each move she made had my attention, and she wasn't doing much but playing in her hair.

"Your bathroom is huge," A'miracle said, as she walked inside the bathroom and turned the light on. I leaned against my dresser and continued to watch her every move. I started drinking from the bottle, never allowing my eyes to leave her flesh. Damn, this girl was fine.

"The tub is deep. I would literally, soak for hours," she said, as she walked out of the bathroom, downed her cup, and proceeded over to me. She was closer than usual. Her body was closer than usual. I could feel the heat radiating from her pores as she looked up at me. Her eyes were like candles in the night, lighting a spark of passion. She licked her lips slowly, as my fingertips explored her.

I could feel the goosebumps scaling her skin. Not the ones you develop when you're frightened or cold. The ones that grace your flesh in excitement, in the heat of the moment, when nothing else matters, except right now, right here. Leaning forward, our noses slightly touching, before our lips finally connected. The kiss was enticing and strong, as my hand went from her cheek to her throat. I squeezed it gently, allowing soft moans to escape her lips. Breaking the kiss, I needed to gain control of this situation. I'm not the type of man to take advantage of a woman while under the influence. If she wanted it, I would never deny her, but I needed her to express that.

"A'miracle, what you doing?" I asked, as her lips kissed my neck. She sucked and bit it gently, causing my shit to swell in my pants. Her scent was intoxicating, more than the Hennessey we drank.

"Please," she begged, as she kissed my lips again. This time, our tongues met. The saliva we exchanged, the way she pressed her body against mine, there was no way I wouldn't grant her request. There was no way I would deny her, I knew I couldn't now. I just needed her to say it.

"Please, I want you to make the pain go away. Just make the pain go away," she gasped, in a voice that made me want her even more. With that being said, I granted her wishes. I kissed her lips again, but this time, with more passion than the first. It felt like a sense of urgency came over me to please her. The chemistry we've developed was indeed undeniable; even in the short period of time we've shared.

As our tongues entwined, I gently laid A'miracle on her back. One by one, our clothes hit the floor, but my eyes never left hers. The lace black bra held her breasts in place, until my lips removed them. I sucked on her nipples, rolling my tongue around her areolas, slightly biting each. My hands trailed her soft flesh, from her neck down to her stomach. I could tell she was nervous, but she wanted it just as bad as I did. Feeling the warmth of her pussy before I even touched it, made my mouth water just thinking about the exotic flavors she possessed.

"Relax," I whispered in her ear, before licking it. In order for me to explore her thoroughly, in order for me to vividly please each and every inch of her, I needed her to relax. In order for me to introduce her mind, body, and soul, to pleasures she'd never experienced before, I needed her to let go of any and all boundaries. I didn't need her approval, because her body would direct me. It would tell me what she could and couldn't take.

The moment she laid down with me, her words were no longer my focus; just her body language. Quickly unbuckling her pants, I tapped her thighs, so she could lift up. Pulling her pants down and off, I smiled at the wet spot that developed between her legs. The seam of her panties was damp from the moisture her pussy provided. Shit like that excited me, especially a woman's exotic scent. Every pussy has its own distinctive smell, and fulfulling taste, and I couldn't wait to devour hers.

Using her pussy as my blank canvas and my tongue as the school of the arts, I illustrated unique images of how her pussy should be eaten. The most delicate piece of flesh, powerful and majestic, was addictive in every sense of the word addiction, and had to be properly nourished. I ate her pussy like a famous Renaissance painter. I ate her pussy like a famous graffiti artist; sculpting swift symmetric tongue twisting tangles of ecstasy. I was a pussy eating bully, and she just became my victim. Illuminating a manuscript with bold italic lettering, I marked my territory on her pussy, with thick scalloped flicks of my tongue. With each one, her moans became louder, and louder. I glanced up at her as she grabbed ahold of the sheets, the pillows, and whatever else she could get on.

I kissed her clit twice, as if I was knocking for her to let me in. I used my tongue to gently open her folds, open her beautiful doors, in which her clit was behind. It welcomed me, she welcomed me, welcomed the warmth of my tongue, and it was the most beautiful sight to see. The most beautiful sight to taste. I slurped her pussy like a 7-11 blueberry slurpy. I kissed it. I sucked it. I licked it in no specific order, as her back started to arch instantly.

"Fuckkk!" A'miracle moaned out, as her legs began to shake. I knew her orgasm was building; I could literally, hear the shit getting ready to gush out. I worked my tongue-terrific magic on her pussy. I inhaled her clit, while making the kissy face at the same time. I sucked her clit like a cherry Starburst. I blew on her clit like I did my morning coffee from Dunkin. I licked her pussy like it was my favorite flavor of ice cream, chocolate. I welcomed her moans, the grinding of her hips, the grinding of her pussy in my face, before her juice box exploded.

"Ahh, I'm cumming, Tabari! Ahh!" She moaned, as her body shook uncontrollably. She tried her best to get away from me, but I wouldn't let her go. It's something about a fight a woman puts up after she came, that I enjoyed the most. My face was wet, my chin was dripping, and I couldn't do shit but smirk at her irregular breathing patterns. Reaching over to my nightstand, I grabbed a condom and slid it on. I placed my dick at her opening, before slowly entering her. I took my time, because I wanted to take mental pictures of her. I wanted to forever remember the face she made when my dick fully coated her walls.

She bit down on her lip as her eyes rolled to the back of her head. I could see the shiny coating on the condom, and hear her juices slapping against my thighs. As the pace sped up, her pussy opened up to me more. Squeezing me as if it was trying to suck me dry. I kissed her lips once more, before wrapping my hand around her neck. I stroked her long and deep, before she squirted all over me. I knew she was probably tired, but I was a beast between the sheets, and I was just getting started.

"Turn that ass over," I demanded, helping her on all fours. I pressed the middle of her back in, making sure her arch was perfect. I entered her quick from behind, and fucked her long and hard.

"Ahh! Fuck, Tabari! This dick bae, shit!" She cried out to me, which was music to my ears. I pulled my dick out and licked the crack of her ass, down to her pussy. I wrapped my lips around her clit again, before trailing back to her ass. I stuck my tongue inside her ass, then bit her booty, before sliding my dick back inside of her; this time, stroking her deeper.

"Ooh, Tabari. I can't take this! I'm cumming again," A'miracle cried out to me. A'miracle was wet as fuck. Literally, the only sounds that echoed off the walls were her moaning and her pussy juices slapping against my thighs. Standing on my tippy toes, I pushed the front of her body down on the bed, tooting her ass up in the air more. Her pussy granted me access even more, and I fucked her like she's never been fucked before. Licking my thumb, I stuck it in her booty, as she came instantly, and I followed right behind her.

"Fuckkk!" I grunted, as the nut shot out from my dick. I pulled my dick out and slid the condom off, as A'miracle fell flat on her face. I slapped her booty before going to the bathroom and getting a warm towel. By the time I cleaned myself up and came back inside the room, I could hear the sounds of light snoring. I softly cleaned her up before pulling her closer to me, and we both fell asleep.

THREE

A'miracle

$\mathcal{I}$ woke up the next morning more relaxed than I've been in days. My spirit was calm, my smile was a little brighter, but most importantly, my mind was at ease. Although I had a lot on my plate at the moment, and what felt like a billion things to do, I still took some time to myself before actually getting my day started. I thought I would have a headache from all the Hennessey we drank last night, but I didn't. I thought I wouldn't remember the events that occurred, but my mind replayed each and every intimate moment we shared.

Tabari took control of my body better than Wade did. I mean, I've never cum so many times in my life, especially after just one session. Usually, I'm ready to go round for round, sex session after sex session. Goes to show that if a nigga really knows what he's doing, and dicking you down right, the only session you need is one. I was so damn high from our encounter last night, that I wasn't even upset that I woke up in his bed alone. I figured he had a ton of things to do, just like me, and we would get at each other later.

After laying in complete bliss for another half hour, I finally pulled myself from his soft sheets and to the bathroom. I started a bath, and checked my phone while the tub filled. I had a message from Eternity, telling me to call her, as well as one from Dove, which seemed a bit odd. I'm sure she finally found out what occurred between her brother and me, and honestly, I didn't know if she had my best interest at heart. I mean, the shit Wade pulled was foul on so many levels, but at the end of the day, he was still her brother, no matter how much she claimed she hated him.

I had a bunch of messages from my mother asking me to meet her, so we could talk. I wasn't sure if I wanted to speak with her or my father just yet. The amount of betrayal I was feeling was unbearable. I've literally, been lied to my entire life, and at 26 years old, finding out your parents aren't your parents is a tough pill to swallow. This shit was definitely playing on my mental, and I'm sure I would need a counselor for this as well. Once the tub filled, I turned on the jets. I couldn't wait to submerge myself inside the warm water and relax. Right before I got in the tub, my phone vibrated, and it was a message from Tabari. I couldn't conceal the smile that spread across my lips at the sight of his name on my screen.

Tabari: *Good morning beautiful. Sorry I had to head out while you were sleeping. You looked so peaceful that I didn't wanna wake you. I'll make it up to you tonight though. How do Netflix's and chill sound? I'll grab snacks, or you can just be mine, your choice...*

I had to squeeze my legs together just thinking about the way he ate my pussy. My God, I was wet from just my thoughts alone. I quickly sent him back the heart eye emoji, and that I would love that, before getting in the tub. My bath lasted well over an hour, since I had a lot on my mind. I need to make a to-do list so that I wouldn't forget any of the important business I had to take care of. Then again, all I wanted to do was climb back in bed and wait for Tabari to arrive.

I know running from my problems, or trying to act like they don't exist, won't help me. I just wasn't sure if I was ready to deal with all this shit. After getting out of the tub and cleaning it out, I found some almond butter lotion on his dresser. I decided to oil my skin with that, and throw on one of his oversize shirts, before heading down to the kitchen. I wanted to raid his refrigerator to see what he had for breakfast. I think I was too damn excited to cook in his kitchen, since it was so big and beautiful.

Walking towards the kitchen, I saw some bags on the dining room table and a note with my name on the front. Picking it up and reading it, I smiled yet again. Tabari was so sweet. He went out and brought me a Puma jogging suit, and matching kicks, since I didn't have any clothes at his house. He even promised to take me shopping, but that won't be necessary. I have too many clothes at home that I haven't worn yet, and don't really need anything else. There was a gun next to the bags with another note. This note said, "take a deep breath, and squeeze the trigger, don't hesitate." It wasn't the first time I held a gun or shot one. I used to hold Wade's guns all the time while we drove around the hood. I guess back then I thought the shit was cute, and didn't know what I was getting myself into. I feel so stupid for fucking with Wade and ignoring the signs.

After looking at the clothes, I went to the kitchen, and over to the microwave. As he stated in the note, he ordered me breakfast, and orange juice was in the refrigerator. I warmed everything up and sat at the table to eat. I texted Eternity back and told her I would meet with her soon, and that I needed a little time to clear my head. I wasn't blowing her off, I just needed time to myself. She also reminded me about the trip we had planned for Miami, and I wasn't sure if I wanted to go. I knew I needed the vacation badly, but I wasn't sure if it was the right time. After finishing breakfast, I headed upstairs to get dressed. I put the gun in my purse, fixed my hair, then went out the door. First stop would be to the insurance company.

"So, let me get this correct, your business was burned to the ground? The police are doing an investigation, and they already know who is responsible?" The breaded white man asked, looking over his glasses. I could tell he wasn't use to not only black people being business owners, but black women. I've explained the entire situation to him for the past hour, not once, but multiple times, and I wasn't about to keep repeating myself.

"Yes, we already established this. What's the next step?" I asked, trying not to sound so upset, but his racist ass was starting to irritate the fuck out of me. I knew my father, well, the man who raised me, always said never let them see you sweat. Never show emotion, or get upset, but I was having a hard time keeping my composure.

"Just a bit more information before I take this to my supervisor. I just need-"

"How about you go get your supervisor since you seem to be having a hard time?" I snapped, just as a woman walked over to us.

"Timothy, I'll handle this. Ms. Evans, right this way," the woman stated leading me to her office. Once inside, she apologized for her colleague and the way he was handling my situation. I explained my situation to her as well. After about twenty minutes of her putting everything in the computer, the look on her face showed that the news she was about to give me wasn't what I wanted to hear.

"Ms. Evans, in situations like this, we do have to do our own investigation as well. I'm not saying that I don't believe you, because I do. I'm sincerely sorry that you're going through this. The only thing I can do right now is cut you a check for three thousand dollars. I know that's not enough to find a building and repurchase everything you've lost, but it's a start. Once the investigation is over, then I will reach out to you and let you know the decision the company has made. Again, I'm truly sorry," the woman said to me. It felt like the wind was knocked from my lungs yet again, and I had to take a moment to get myself together. Not only did I lose everything, now that I'm back at square one, I wasn't sure how to dig myself out of this hole.

"Thank you. I appreciate it," I said, trying to sound grateful, but I didn't feel that way. After signing the last of the paperwork, she handed me the envelope with the check for three thousand dollars. I thanked her and made my way back to the car and to the bank to deposit it. It was well into the afternoon, and I hadn't eaten anything.

All the stress was taking a toll on me, and affecting my eating habits. My phone vibrated, and it was a message from my mother, begging me to come to the house and speak with her. As bad as I didn't wanna go, I couldn't stop myself from driving in the direction of the house. I felt like I deserved an explanation, I needed an explanation from her. She needed to explain this shit to her child, to me. She was the only mother I knew of, the only mother I had. None of this made any sense, and honestly, I felt like it was her job to make this shit make sense. I fucking deserved that much!

I wasn't sure how this conversation would go, but the closer I got to the house, the more anxious I became. I got out of the car and walked inside. As usual, I slipped my shoes off and my mother was waiting for me in the living room. For a moment, neither of us said anything. We both just stood there quietly looking at each other. Usually, I would be excited to see her, excited to wrap my arms around my mother, but now, I didn't know what to feel.

"A'miracle, please, let's sit down," my mother suggested, patting the seat next to her. I took a seat as I've always done, pulling my feet underneath me. My nerves were all over the place, I found myself twirling my thumbs. My hands were shaking, and it felt like my heart was beating a million miles a minute. She tried to console me, but I quickly moved my hands away. I wasn't trying to be rude, I just didn't feel like being touched. My emotions were overflowing. My mind was a million and one places, and the only thing I wanted was answers. I needed answers.

"A'miracle, I-"

"Please, Mom, I mean, Melissa, right?" I spat, pointing at her before she could say anything else. I knew that comment pissed her off, and I wanted it to. I wanted her to feel everything I was feeling. I wanted her to hurt like me.

"Don't start with I'm sorry. Just tell me, why?" I asked, pulling my hair behind my ears as my voice cracked.

"The situation is difficult. A'miracle, we never wanted you to find out this way," my mother said, causing me to get upset.

"You never wanted me to find out this way, or was it that you never meant for me to find out at all?" I asked, looking at her. I could see the tears welling up in her eyes, and it only pissed me off more. How could she be upset, when I'm the one who's been lied to my entire fucking life? Before I knew it, I snapped.

"No! Don't do that! You don't get to cry, Mom! You don't get to shed one fucking tear!" I yelled, standing to my feet.

"A'miracle! Would you please just listen to me?!" My mother pleaded, as she grabbed my arm.

"It wasn't that we didn't wanna tell you, A'miracle. We just didn't know how. I-"

"Oh, so a simple, 'hey, A'miracle, you're actually adopted, and we're not your biological parents,' couldn't have worked?" I yelled, cutting her off, and allowing my emotions to get the best of me. I was so mad that I was shaking.

"Instead, I had to find out through a fucking doctor, who clearly violated HIPPA, that I'm not your kid! Do you know how that makes me feel? Can you imagine how I feel inside?" I asked, jerking away from her, and wiping away the tears that managed to escape.

"We didn't mean to hurt you, A'miracle. Please, just sit down and listen to me, I'm begging you," my mother cried. Walking back over to her, I took a seat. I told myself that I would listen to what she has to say, even though my heart felt like things would only get worse.

"I remember being happy when I found out I was pregnant. Literally, everything was so perfect. I had the perfect man, who had the perfect job, and together, we would raise the perfect family. At least, that's what I thought. Nothing was wrong, nothing, at all. I mean, I did exactly what the doctors told me to do. I took those big ass vitamins, daily, I went to all the doctor's appointments; never missed one. The baby's heartbeat was strong, so strong. I did every-thing right, I swear, I did," my mother explained, looking over at me. As the tears rolled down her face, I've never seen her so hurt. I've never seen her this way before. Granted, I've seen her cry, but nothing like this. Something was wrong; something about this story she was sharing with me was wrong.

"I remember having pains, and I brushed it off, thinking it was normal. The next morning, the pains got a lot worse, and I was bleeding a little. Your father took me to the hospital immediately.

They kept searching, and searching, but they couldn't find my baby's heartbeat. I had to deliver my baby, knowing that I would never hear her small cries. I had to push my baby out, knowing that my daughter was already dead. I went through the entire delivery, felt the contractions, cried from the pain, knowing that I would never be a mother," my mother cried.

"I remember the doctor saying she was out, and hearing the sound of the room after she was born. It was so silent, so sad. It was like I was waiting for her to cry. I was begging God to let the doctors be wrong, and for my baby to just cry, but it never happened. I cried so bad, and some of the nurses did too. I was able to hold her and take pictures of her, but it wasn't the same. I knew that no amount of kisses, no amount of hugs, no amount of tears, or pleas, would allow her to breathe and come home with me. I was depressed for months, I blamed myself. I was suicidal, and wanted to end my life at times. I wouldn't wish this feeling on my worst enemy. I still think about her every day, and wonder what her voice sounds like, her laugh. What would be her favorite food and things she would love to do. Our marriage got rocky because of the mental state I was in. No matter how hard I tried, I couldn't shake it, I couldn't. I went to counseling, took medications, and it didn't work. I still felt the same," my mother went on, causing me to feel extremely bad. My heart ached for my mother. She's never shared this with me, and we were like best friends. She was more than a mother to me, and at some point, I could talk to her about anything. I regret not speaking to her off the fact that I chose my relationship over her too. I can only imagine how she felt, and she really needed me, and I let her down.

"Mom, I'm-"

"No, let me finish this," my mother pleaded, as she reached for my hand. This time, I held it.

"I remember getting the divorce papers from my lawyer. I didn't want them delivered to your father; instead, I wanted to give them to him myself and give him the explanation he deserved. I felt like I was broken as a woman. I felt like I was broken as his wife. By not being able to provide him with the one thing he has ever asked of me, and that's to bear his children. I couldn't do it, A'miracle. I felt helpless, and I also felt as if I was holding him back from the life he deserved. I dreamed of letting your father go, and him finding the perfect woman to give him a bunch of babies. The night that I went to the fire station to give him the papers, it was cold out. Once I gave him the papers, I planned to go home and kill myself. I had already written a letter, and had the pill mixture waiting for me by the bed. I knew that he wouldn't come home until late, and by the time he did, I would be dead. I had a plan, and you changed that," my mother said to me.

"I remember parking in the lot and walking around to the front. As I got closer, I heard something. I heard the sound of crying, and I couldn't believe my eyes. There was a baby outside of the door, and that baby was you," my mother said to me, causing me to gasp, covering my mouth.

"I remember using his code to get inside of the station, and picking you up out of the box you were in. I don't know what happened to me, but my motherly instincts kicked right in. I remember the look on your father's face when he saw me holding you. You were so small, and a bit dirty. You really looked like you'd been through hell when I held you in my arms. I remember thinking, who wouldn't want someone so precious? Even through the blood and the dirt, you were absolutely the prettiest baby girl I've ever seen. Your father was at a loss for words. He really thought I've lost the little mind I had left, and took someone's child," my mother said, laughing a little.

"Once I explained what happened to him, we took you to the hospital, just to make sure you were ok. By your father being a fireman at the time, he knew a lot of people. He called a nurse he could trust to help us, and you've been with us every since. Back then, it was so many babies abandoned, that the courts literally gave you to us, no questions asked. They were happy that a family actually stepped up to provide a life for a child, when their biological parents decided not to. This mark on your arm, it wasn't your birthmark," my mother said to me, touching my arm. I looked back and forth from the scar to my mother, waiting on her to explain.

"You were severely burned, A'miracle; from what, I have no idea. With the creams and antibiotics, I made sure you didn't catch any infections, and it healed like this. I took care of you, A'miracle. I took good care of you like I gave birth to you myself. That night you had my whole heart, not just pieces of it, but all of it. I've never loved someone as much as I love you. I believe you were sent from God to me. You were a miracle, baby girl, my miracle baby, and that's why I named you A'miracle. I saved your life, and in return, you saved mine," my mother said, causing me to cry even harder.

"Our intentions were never meant to hurt you. We should have told you, and for that, I take the full blame. Your father wanted to tell you, but I didn't. I kept putting things off, and telling him now wasn't the time. Honestly, the time would never be right for us to tell you something like that. As your mother, I guess I wanted to protect you. I'm sorry I let you down," my mother said, hugging me while I continued to cry in her arms.

"I kept it all, everything, because I knew one day, I would have this conversation with you. It's all here in this box. Your father thought I was crazy for keeping something like this around, but I couldn't throw it away. I really don't know why I couldn't, but I kept it," my mother said, picking up the box from the table. It looked like a small chest, that was purple, with clear stones around it.

"Ma, I can't open this right now. I just can't," I cried.

"Then don't. Open it when you feel like the time is right. It's not much in there that could help you, but it's a start," my mother said, hugging me once more. I felt so lost, and my feelings were hurt. I wasn't mad that they adopted me, actually, I was blessed that they did. So many children nowadays are losing their lives, because their parents can't properly give them the love they need. So, I'm grateful for my adoptive parents, but that still didn't stop me from wondering where my biological parents were. I mean, I would love to know what was so damn bad about me that they let me go. I wanted to know what really happened that night, since I've only heard one story. I was saddened that my family abandoned me more than anything. How could you just hold a baby for nine months, and decided one day you don't wanna be a parent anymore? I stayed with my mother for a while, and we both just cried and consoled one another. God knows when it rains, it definitely pours. As bad as I wanted to know who my real parents were, I was starting to wonder, was it worth it? I mean, when you go searching for things, you definitely will find them, and when you ask you shall receive. The only problem is, would I honestly be ok with whatever I found? Can I honestly accept it no matter how good, no matter how bad? Would I be able to open this box and accept whatever was inside?

FOUR

Tabari

$\mathcal{I}$t wasn't my intentions to be gone when A'miracle woke up, but a nigga had business to take care of. With the night we just shared, I could have basked in the feeling of having her next to me forever. I could have basked in her warmth, her sweetness, but most importantly, I could have basked in her pussy for days to come. Crazy as it sounds, now I see why the nigga Wade was losing all his marbles over her. Women really don't know the power they hold between their legs. It's already hard to find faithful, good pussy, but to have brains and beauty to match, had me ready to marry A'miracle's ass.

Shaking last night's thoughts from my head, I had to stay focused, and keep my head in the game. When Choppa hit me up and told me to meet him this afternoon, I decided to get up early to grab A'miracle a few things. I knew this had to be hard on her, since it felt like her entire life was in shambles in a matter of days. I wanted to make things as easy as I could for her, all while protecting her. A'miracle was strong, so I wasn't worried about her not being able to handle the gun I left. If I couldn't be with her every minute of the day, I needed to know that she had something to protect herself with. My car was bulletproof; something my uncle lived by, so I knew A'miracle would be safe driving it. I didn't tell her that since I didn't want to scare her. She didn't look like the type of woman to really fuck with a street nigga on a level like this, so the last thing I needed was to run her away. All I wanted to do was protect her, since she's growing on me and I care about her. So hopefully, she didn't mind, and understood exactly where I was coming from.

Once I got a rental, I stopped by to see my mom and sister for a brief moment. They both were doing fine, and my mother had an old friend from school stop by. The woman's eyes looked familiar, but I wasn't sure where I saw her before. I mean, her appearance was nothing compared to the circumstances she endured. She was a sweet woman, and still beautiful; at least that's what my mother said. She spoke so highly about Fe-Fe, and explained her terrible situation. She was definitely a living miracle. They've been friends for a while, lost touch at one point, but they somehow found their way back to each other. It felt good to see my mother talking and laughing, instead of in pain. She deserved to be happy and be surrounded by people who care for her. Although I knew my mother's condition, I still hoped and prayed she would bounce back fully one day.

I said my goodbyes to Fe-Fe and my mother, and promised my sister I'd be back soon, before I headed to the address Choppa gave me. I could feel myself changing into the man my uncle never wanted me to be, and I welcomed it. I knew things were about to get worse, and I had to figure out a way to convince my mother to go away on a trip. I didn't know where I would send her, but I needed her safe. The last thing I needed was to lose those closest to me, by trying to get revenge for my uncle's death. I knew if my mother found out what I was up to, I would be a huge disappointment to her, and she would try to talk me out of it. It's just certain shit I couldn't let go of, and this was one of them. I pulled into the parking lot of *Regal Inn* located in Franklin Park. It was a run-down hotel that prostitutes usually work out of, and drug transactions took place. I knew all of this because of my uncle. Crazy how he used to think I wasn't listening to him, and I remembered everything he's ever taught me. I got out of the car and checked my surroundings before heading up to the room. I knocked twice as instructed, before the door opened.

"Bear, right?" The dread head said, standing in front of me. I was too busy looking at all of the artillery scattered all over the bed, that I didn't respond.

"You good, lil nigga?" The guy standing before me, stated in a voice that broke me from the trance I was in.

"Yea, yea, I'm sorry, man. I'm Bear," I said, shaking his hand as he closed and locked the door.

"So, what's the game plan?" I said, taking a seat in the chair over in the corner. Spade laughed as he picked up one of the guns and loaded it. I didn't know what the fuck was funny, but buddy was giving me a bad vibe.

"You do realize this isn't a game? The shit we about to do isn't a game. Wrong choice of words, lil nigga," Spade said, causing me to bite the inside of my jaw. I don't know if this was a scare tactic or what, but buddy's ass was in for a rude awakening, if he didn't calm all the shit down.

"Bear, what do you know about this nigga?" Choppa asked, smoking a blunt. The nigga looked much bigger in person. His entire demeanor was calm, but demanded respect. I can see why my uncle fucked with him. He was definitely about his business. The fact that he came all the way to the Chi, just based on his loyalty and friendship with my uncle gained my respect; period.

"Lazer not your typical nigga. He not even a shooter. He doesn't fuck with drugs or anything like that. That's not his line of work. He murks motherfuckers for a living. Kills motherfuckers in the worse way, and leaves no trace. He lives in K-town. You would think a motherfucker like him would rest his head somewhere outside of the hood, but nope, not him. Guess you can't take the hood out of everybody," I said, honestly, looking at their expressions change.

"So, this nigga's an assassin?" Choppa asked.

"Yea, a hood one though. Majority of his work is done with machetes, big ass knives, and shit. That's why it doesn't make sense that he's the one behind my uncle's death, especially when he was shot," I replied, causing them both to look back and forth at each other.

"You got a team? Well, I know you don't have one, or else we wouldn't be here," Spade said, shaking his head, causing me to snap.

"Aye, nigga, what's your problem, fam? I ain't into all that shit you talking, fam. I got enough on my plate right now, unless you trying to become a side dish. The choice is yours," I grunted, standing, and eyeing the nigga. We didn't say shit for a moment, just felt each other out, before he eventually started laughing. I knew then that this motherfucker was crazy.

"Yea, now that's the nigga we need!" Spade yelled, confusing the hell out of me.

"Keep his ass out, because this shit is about to get ugly, fam; real ugly. I'm just fucking with you, Bear. Just had to make sure you weren't a bitch, you feel me?" He asked, causing me to nod.

"Can't have a big ass shootout and start a fucking war with a motherfucker that would cry in the car. Can't fuck with no niggas that'll freeze up either. You passed my lil test, you good," Spade said, reaching his hand out for me to shake.

"Now, let's get down to business. You got anybody else you can trust? Someone who will know his moves? How he operates?" Choppa asked, causing me to think long in hard. Since I really wasn't apart of the streets like that, I really didn't know who to trust, except the lil niggas that proved to be down for me. They knew more about this nigga than I did.

"I can get you bout' two or three more people that I can actually vouch for. Everybody else gone," I said, looking at Choppa.

"Yea, typical nigga shit. When the shit hit the fan, mother-fuckers always jump ship. It's cool though. I'll handle it, and get you a fresh team; some trill ass niggas. You gonna need them when this is over, and I'm gone. Call them niggas up though, tell them to meet us," Choppa said, standing, and putting on a vest before tossing one my way.

"Meet us where, fam?" I asked, as I slipped it on.

"West, nigga, you said the niggas we about to murk live in K-town," Spade said, passing the blunt to me. Once I strapped the vest up, I hit the blunt a few times before passing it over to Choppa.

"You can handle this?" Choppa said, pointing to one of the AK's.

"Hell, yea," I responded, picking it up.

"Aight, let's roll," Choppa stated, picking up his choice of weapons before we headed out the door. Spade put two duffle bags in the back of the Tahoe truck that was parked next to mine. Once inside, I hit up Tazz and put him up on game, and told him where to meet us. Once we all were together, we headed towards K-town. Choppa explained that we needed to find out as much as we could in a short period of time. Something that would usually take a month to do plenty of homework on, we were squeezing into forty-eight hours; seventy-two tops. Choppa literally, taught us a bunch of shit we didn't know; basically, putting us up on the game. To my understanding, Choppa never liked Wade and could see right through Wade's actions. It made me wonder how my uncle couldn't see that this nigga was a snake.

"Anything yet?" Choppa asked, as I looked at my phone waiting for a message from Meechie. This lil nigga was all over the place, and knew damn near everything. He told me he would send me the location that Lazer was at, since he knew a couple of niggas that worked with him. Meechie couldn't be trusted, and he knew this. I was just keeping the little nigga around for information. Yea, he told me who killed my uncle, but the little nigga still couldn't be trusted in my eyes. It's only a matter of time before his family would be burying him. It's sad, but true. Before I could respond to Choppa, my phone vibrated a few times. It was screenshots of Lazer's Facebook profile. The pictures were basically Lazer checking in at this club called S2. It confused me for a second, until Tazz's phone vibrated, and it was a FaceTime call from Meechie.

"Aye, what's up?" Tazz said, as he answered.

"Ok, listen, the pictures I just sent to Tabari's phone is Lazer's profile. But here's the thing, he has always checked in at that club on Wednesdays. I mean, I had one of my lil bitch searching his page for me, and the posts go back to last summer. This nigga is really there popping bottles and shit, every Wednesday. Since today is Wednesday, I'll bet everything I have that his ass will be there," Meechie explained.

"Aight, good looking out," Tazz said, ending the call. I Googled the address, and we headed in that direction. My hands were itching to kill this motherfucker. My uncle didn't deserve that shit, and I wasn't a killer, but today I will be. We parked across the street a block back, and watched our surroundings. From the view we had, we could see who came into the club and left out. Bitches were out in the shortest shit, long weaves, and heels. The line was down the block, and it actually looked like the spot to be on a Wednesday night. I would have to holla at Keahi and tell him about this spot since he just opened his bar. This is the type of traffic he needs to really get his bar up and running.

By now, we had smoked about three blunts, and I wasn't as nervous as I thought I would be. Spade's high ass was cracking jokes as we waited for our target. While those motherfuckers were talking, I decided to send A'miracle a text to check on her, and to tell her that I would be home soon. Her reads were on, so I knew she saw my message, but she didn't reply. I figured she was probably busy doing something, so I blew it off and focused my attention on the crowd that was walking towards the door.

"Looks like we got action," I said, as I sat up in my seat making sure my eyes weren't playing tricks on me. Lazer was walking towards the door with his entourage. He was in the front with about six niggas behind him. Everything in me was telling me to get out of the car and to kill this nigga exactly where he stood, but I knew that would only make matters worse.

"That's his ass, right?" Choppa asked, looking back at me.

"Yea, that's him," I responded, waiting for him to tell us what the next move is.

"Aight, looks like we going to join the party," Choppa said, turning off the truck and getting out of the car. Spade walked to the back and opened the duffle bag that held a bunch of handguns. I quickly grabbed two Glocks and placed one on my side and the other on my back. I made sure my shirt was covering my vest. We walked towards the door and straight through security. I didn't know Choppa had pull like that, since they literally, just let us in; not even searching us. Choppa shook up with the security pulled one of the bottle girls to the side, and whispered something in her ear. Moments later, she guided us up the stairs and to a VIP section. From the outside looking in, you wouldn't think this place was so big inside. The top floor was mainly sectioned, and gave us the perfect view of the club. I spotted Lazer's ass at the bottom, in the corner with his people. Bitches were breaking their necks to get over to him and his guys. Soon as the new Cardi B song blasted through the speakers, bitches were shaking more ass than Magic City. Money was flying in the air, and these niggas were really acting as if they were at the strip club. Drinking, smoking, and lacking hard as fuck, is the quickest way for the enemy to get you. Little did they know, they were making things so much easier. I was just waiting on word from Choppa to air this bitch out.

FIVE

A'miracle

———————

$\mathcal{I}$ really wasn't in a good mood after I left my mother's house. I honestly didn't know how to channel my emotions, or even explain them at this point. My entire life is in shambles. Literally, everything I thought I knew about who I am was a lie. I will never be the same after this. Twenty-six years old, and finding out you're adopted, and the family who raised you isn't yours, is difficult to accept. Although I just spoke to my mother, well my adoptive mother, my heart goes out to her. I didn't know she had a difficult time conceiving, and I basically saved her life and marriage. I was still confused though. Honestly, I had so many unanswered questions, that I'm sure she couldn't help me with.

I wanted to know who my biological parents were. Hell, if they still were alive. I wanted to know what my name was before A'miracle. Any little detail that would help me accept something that I have no control over, and give me the ability to keep going. I glanced over at the box that was on the passenger side floor. I was anxious to see what was inside, but on the other hand, I was scared. God knows I wanted to give up right now, and I needed His guidance more than anything. Oddly, I felt like I was starting to lose my parents, and this was my second set, if that makes sense. My adoptive father needed a kidney transplant, and it's not a guarantee he will receive one. I know how the system works, and how long the transplant lists are. My adoptive mother was so depressed, that she was actually scaring me. I didn't want anything to happen to either one of them, but I knew if my adoptive father died, Melissa wouldn't be able to handle it. Neither would I. He was my Superman. My father was everything to me, even when we fell apart. I knew if I ever needed him, despite his cold heart, he would be right there by my side. So, he needed me, and I had to be there for him, even if I didn't know the outcome.

Thinking about everything, I truly didn't know why my parents made the decision that they did. What hurts the most was the fact that they didn't even take me to an adoption agency; not even a hospital. They literally, left me in a brown box, outside of a fire station, in the middle of the winter. Why didn't they make sure I was safe? Anything could have happened to me. That's something I will never get over, or be able to accept. Yes, I'm grateful that God allowed Melissa to come to the fire station that night, but what would have happened if she didn't? Would anyone have come for me? Would anyone have heard my small cries, and come to my aid? Just thinking about the fact that there could have been a chance that I would have died out there, made me even more thankful for my adoptive parents.

Making it back to the city, I decided to drive by my place. It looked normal, and my car was still there. I drove around the block again before I parked Tabari's car in front of my car and got out. I wanted to grab some important paperwork from my safe, and get anything out of my car I may need. Unlocking my car door, I locked myself inside and went through my glove box. I don't know why my heart was beating so fast, but it was. I had to take a brief moment to calm myself so that I could focus. Nothing was inside that I thought I needed, so I closed it and pulled my visors down. The paperwork from the hospital fell in my lap, and I couldn't help but look at the therapist information. Maybe it would be a good time to set some appointments and actually go. I felt like I was dealing with a lot, and maybe a trained professional would be able to help me. I took the paperwork and got out of the car. I quickly unlocked my front door and walked inside; locking it behind me. Everything still was in place. It looked the same as I left it, but I couldn't help the eerie feeling that came over me.

All the memories came crashing back as I got closer to my room. I remembered everything Wade did to me. I remember how his fist connected with my flesh. I remember how his eyes looked, and the horrible things he said to me. I remember crying and begging him to stop, and he never did. I lost part of me that day; a part of me that I will never get back. I went over to my closet and grabbed my suitcase. It was already filled with clothes, but those were for the trip to Miami. Since I wasn't going anymore, I needed to repack. Not wanting to be here long, I just emptied everything on the bed and packed a bunch of jeans, leggings, and shirts. I grabbed a couple of pairs of shoes, and even a few heels and dresses, just in case I went on a date with Tabari. He was so sweet. I loved the way he just wanted to make sure I was ok, and the fact that he invited me into his world. I knew this man had a million things to do. He would make any woman happy, and here he was, simply taking care of me and making me smile. My phone vibrated as I zipped my suitcase. It was Dove, and I wondered what was she calling for. We didn't fall out, but at the end of the day, Wade was still her brother. I decided not to answer it, and grabbed my favorite toiletries from my bathroom. Once I knew I had everything, including the paperwork that was in the safe, and my MacBook, I decided I spent enough time here, and I needed to head back to Tabari's. The last thing I needed was to run into Wade or Lazer. Walking back to the front door, I damn near screamed when I opened it to find Dove standing there.

"Damn, you scared the shit out of me," I barked, looking at her ass like she was crazy.

"I'm sorry. I called and you didn't answer. I saw your car, so I figured I would come up," she said, looking around, trying to see who was in my house. That shit threw me completely off.

"So, let me guess, you're here on Wade's behalf?" I asked, leaning against my door. I could tell something was wrong with her, but I didn't bother asking. I hated her brother for what he did to me, and if she couldn't understand that, then we no longer needed to be friends.

"No, I'm not. I haven't seen him. I'm sorry about what happened, and what he did to you," Dove moaned, sympathetically, but I didn't believe her. Instead of entertaining this conversation, I politely pulled my suitcase into the hallway and locked my door. I wasn't trying to come off rude, but I really didn't feel like speaking to him, her, or anyone involved with Wade's ass.

"Listen, I'm not trying to be rude or anything, but I have some things I have to take care of. So, what's your reason for being here?" I finally asked, trying to get to the root of this conversation.

"A'miracle, regardless of everything, you're still my friend. I still love, and only want the best for you, and that's not my brother. Listen, I'll shoot you an address later, since I know you have some things you need to handle. I don't wanna hold you up, because I have to handle things too. Can you please just come out and talk to me? Please, what I have to say you will want to hear. Just trust me," Dove explained, hugging me, and walking away. I stood there for a moment, wondering what the hell just happened. What did she mean by what she had to tell me I needed to hear? Shrugging, I double checked to make sure my door was locked before I headed down to Tabari's car. At this point, I wanted to get the hell from over there. If she popped up on me like this, then I knew it was only a matter of time before Wade showed his face again. I didn't have time for any of the shit.

Once everything was packed into the trunk, I got in Tabari's car, and damn near did the dash back to his place. Seeing her made my anxiety act up. I mean, Dove seemed normal, but why did I have to meet her to talk? Why couldn't she just tell me while we were face to face? Something about this situation didn't seem too good. I put all of my things in the corner of Tabari's room when I made it back to his place, before taking a quick shower and ordering something to eat. I knew I had a lot of emails to return. I needed to finally contact my clients, call my assistant, and get back in businesswoman mode. Everything that was happening was taking a toll on me, but I've worked too damn hard to let it end my career. My bills are still going to need paying, and I have an image to uphold. I'm sure my assistant, Nicole, was worried sick, since I haven't spoken to her. She was as loyal as they came, and texted me every other day to check on me. She was a sweetheart, and I definitely owed her a phone call. Once I handled things with my assistant, I moved on to my clients and sent out a boatload of emails. Most of my clients were understanding to the fact that things will be delayed for at least another week. The only one who was giving me problems was Mr. Martinez. He was such an asshole. At this point, I was ready to just refund him his money, and let the smart mouth bastard go on about his business. I didn't need that type of negativity in my life.

I didn't wanna ask my mother for money, because I knew she had a lot on her plate with my father. There's no telling which way things are going to play out, plus, insurance only pays for so much. Tabari has already done enough, and there was no way I was asking him either. I will take this as a lessoned learned, and pray the insurance company finds in my favor, and cut me a real check. Laying across the bed, I decided to FaceTime Eternity. I felt like I've been blowing my best friend off, and I'm sure she's worried about me. The phone rang about three times before she answered. It felt good just getting things off my chest with her. Eternity was never the type to judge any of the decisions I made, but she would call you out on bullshit. Those are the types of friends you needed.

We chatted for a little over a half hour before Dove texted me. She sent me her location and begged me to meet her. When I told Eternity what happened, she was all for the meeting, and even told me she would come to pick me up and drive there. That's why I loved that damn girl. She was down to ride, no matter the cause. Since I had already showered, it didn't take me long to get ready. I decided to wear a pair of grey leggings, and a red sweater. Chicago weather could be tricky, plus, I'm always cold. I had no idea what place this was, but I was dressed casually. I guess great minds think alike, because Eternity was dressed casually too, but more on the sexy side. This damn girl didn't care about the degrees outside; if she wanted to put on a dress, she would. It wasn't fully fitted, but the cream dress flowed out around the waist. She paired it with a blue jean jacket, and a pair of brown knee boots. We both were cute, as we headed to some place called S2. When we got there and finally found a park, I wanted to turn around so bad. Dove knows we don't do clubs and the loud ass music, bitches standing outside, and the fact the line was down the damn street, threw me off.

"I'm not feeling this shit. We should have Googled this before driving all the way over here," I complained, as we headed towards the door. I don't know what Dove had going on, but she sent me some type of code to show the people at the door, so we wouldn't have to wait in line. That was cool in all, but I still had an attitude, because I didn't like this type of scenery.

I showed the buff man at the door my phone, and he scanned it, and let us in. We walked up to security to get searched, but a couple of bitches were acting crazy by the bar, that he waved us through after taking a few mental pictures of us. He damn near was drooling, which made Eternity laugh, but my stomach turned. I was glad that he waved us through, since I still had the gun in my purse, and completely forgot about it. The last thing I needed was to get arrested. This place was packed from wall to wall, as we made our way over in the direction Dove told us to walk. She was sitting down on the sofa when we made our way over. Her face turned when she saw Eternity, but she quickly brushed that shit off; not quick enough though, since I picked up on it. She gave us both a quick hug before we took a seat. There were juices already there with a bucket of ice. At this point, I didn't even know if I wanted to drink. I needed to watch my surroundings and be alert. Then again, I didn't know what this conversation was about, or how it would go, so I needed something to take the edge off. One of the bottle girls walked over with that sparkly thing and a bottle of Hennessey. Of course, people had to turn and see who was popping bottles. My phone vibrated just in time, since I didn't want people just staring at me, plus, it was a message from Tabari. I read over it, and was about to reply, until Dove started tripping.

"I didn't know you were bringing Eternity with you," Dove said, which threw us both off. I knew this conversation was going left, so I focused my attention on the bottle girl as she opened the bottle for us. I told her to give it to me straight, with two cubes of ice. I didn't even want any juice at this point, since I had to calm my nerves down.

"Why wouldn't she bring me? I mean, after all, this is a club," Eternity snapped, dismissing Dove, and telling the bottle girl how to make her drink. The entire time I looked at Dove, her vibe was off. She kept looking over her shoulder, as if she was hiding from someone. She kept shaking her legs, and clasping her hands together, as if she was silently praying. Her entire demeanor was completely off, and it concerned me. I knew one thing, if Wade's ass popped up, and she had anything to do with it, I was liable to beat the shit out of both of them. I didn't wanna fix anything with that man, and did I want to see him. For Dove's sake, I prayed Wade didn't show up, or this will be the end of our friendship for sure. Not wanting to act a fool, I drank the majority of my drink before I spoke to her.

"Dove, what did you wanna tell me?" I asked, as calmly as I could. I could tell Eternity was on ten, and knew it was taking everything in her not to slap the fuck out of Dove. Dove had a smart-ass mouth, and Eternity had hands for days. She was definitely not the one to fuck with.

"I wanted to talk to you privately, I-"

"You know what, Dove, fuck you! Whatever you have to say to her, you can say while I'm here. Since when do we hold secrets? Unless this has something to do with that bitch ass brother of yours," Eternity snapped, taking her purse and moving it to the side. I knew then things were about to get messy, and I had to do something to stop it.

"Listen, calm down. All I'm asking is, why did you bring me to a loud ass club to talk? How are we going to hear each other?" I tried to yell over the music.

"It needed to be someplace public, where a lot of people are. I'm trying to protect you, A'miracle," Dove yelled back to me, standing, causing me to stand with her. Her voice cracked, and she looked like she was on the verge of a nervous breakdown. I haven't seen her like this in a while. Whenever she does get like this, it's because of thoughts of her mother, or the things she experienced growing up. I tried to touch her to reassure her that things were ok, and she just needed to tell me what was wrong, but she jerked away from me.

"You know, maybe this isn't a good idea. I think we should leave," Dove said, as she looked around. I didn't know who she was looking for, but the shit was creeping me out. I watched as she excused herself, and walked away from us, which only pissed me off more. I grabbed my purse, and Eternity and went after her. It was crowded, so Dove couldn't get far, and the moment she was in arms width, I yanked her ass, and made her turn to face me. Her face was filled with tears, and I had no idea why she was crying.

"What is going on with you, Dove? You're acting crazy! First, you pop up at my place telling me you needed to talk to me. Now that I'm here at a fucking club that you picked, you don't wanna talk anymore? On top of that, you snapping on Eternity and saying smart ass shit like we don't tell each other everything! What the fuck is going on?" I yelled, causing a few of the people standing around us to focus their attention on us. Out of the corner of my eye, I saw a bunch of money on the floor; trailing up to another VIP section. Looking back at Dove, it was like all of the blood literally, left her face. I followed her eyes, and I damn near jumped out of my skin when I saw who she was looking at. Lazer was sitting there looking at us both, and before I knew it, he was to his feet and walking over to us.

"I'm sorry, A'miracle. I'm so sorry," Dove said, trying to grab a hold of my hand. I yanked it away from her, realizing this shit was just a setup. How could she do something like this to me?

"Bitch, I should fucking kill you!" I yelled, fumbling around in my purse for the gun. I couldn't even pull it out in time, before I heard shots behind me. Instantly, people started screaming and running in all directions, and I stood frozen, never taking my eyes of Laser. He wrapped his arm around Dove's neck, just as I felt a pair of hands grabbing me. I looked back, and it was Tabari, pulling me backward in his direction. I started screaming, because I couldn't leave Eternity. She ran over to me, and another man grabbed her, as more guns were drawn. Lazer had a sinister grin on his face, as he placed a knife to Dove's throat. He licked her face, before he pulled it across, from one side to the next. I watched as blood shot out of Dove's neck and mouth, as the tears continued to roll down her face. It happened so fast, and I couldn't believe what I was witnessing. Life left Dove's body, as she hit the floor in a loud thump.

By now, I was screaming and hollering, and Tabari was doing his best to get me and Eternity out of there. Lazer ran towards the back, as shots were going off in all directions. You could literally, hear them bouncing off things around us, as we ducked and dodged them. Once the cool air hit my skin, Tabari told us to run, and we took off towards the parking lot. It was a madhouse, with people running from car to car trying to get out of there. Tabari guided us over to a truck that was parked on the street, and pushed us down behind it. I watched as he pulled guns out, and ran back in the direction we just came from.

"Tabari, no!" I screamed, damn near running after him, but Eternity grabbed me. Eternity hugged me as we both cried together.

"He killed her! He killed her!" Eternity cried, as her eyes got bigger, and bigger. I tried my best to calm her down, but I knew it was no use. I knew this only brought back memories of her mother, since her mother was killed in Atlanta. The sad part is, her mother's throat was slit as well.

"We're ok! We're ok!" I said, grabbing her, and pulling her head to my chest. There was so much commotion going on around us, and I prayed Tabari came back soon. All I wanted to do was get the hell away from this shit. I can't believe Lazer killed Dove like that. Why would he do that? Is it because he can't get to Wade? Is that why Dove said she wanted to talk to me, so we could be in the same spot? So many questions were running through my head, and I had no answers to them. Lazer literally, slit her throat right in front of me, with a smile on his face. Who could be so damn heartless? Is that something I had to look forward to, all because of my dealing with Wade? Regardless of us being into it, Dove didn't deserve that shit! She didn't. I heard cars speeding off, and more shots, before a bunch of footsteps.

"Get in, bae!" Tabari yelled, opening the door for us.

"Wait, my car! I can't leave my car!" Eternity screamed, pointing to the parking lot.

"Give me your keys!" A guy yelled, holding his hand out. Eternity didn't hesitate giving it to him, as we watched him run across the street and to the parking lot. We both got inside the truck and waited for the guy to return with Eternity's car. Shaking as the car filled with a bunch of men we didn't know, I could tell Tabari was mad. I didn't know if he was mad at me, or mad that things happened in front of me. Tabari pulled me on to his lap and held me, while I held Eternity's hand. I cried so bad on his shoulder, that I was sure I would have to replace his shirt. A knock at the window startled me, and it was the guy with Eternity's car. Instantly, we got out and got inside the car.

"Aye, take care of your lady, man, and I'll hit you up in a few," a man with dreads said to Tabari, as he strapped both me and Eternity in the backseat.

"Aight, Choppa," Tabari said, as he hoped in the driver seat. Soon as the doors closed, Tabari sped off. I could see blood on his hands, and wondered if she was ok. Things can't be this fucking crazy in my life, they just couldn't be! It felt like I was in an ongoing nightmare that I couldn't wake up from.

"A'miracle! Bae, I need you to keep it together for me. I will handle this shit," Tabari growled, picking up his phone and making a call.

"Aye, Keahi, meet me at my place, fam. Leave now, it's an emergency," Tabari said, as he made a quick right turn. He finally slowed down enough and put his seatbelt on. He continued to look in the rearview mirror to make sure no one was following us. My heart was beating so fast, and I knew I was on the verge of having an anxiety attack.

"We'll be home soon, bae. Just close your eyes and breathe," he said to me, and I did. I was shaking so bad. Eternity was shaking, and we both were fucked up. When we pulled up to Tabari house, Keahi was standing outside, and rushed over to us. Keahi unbuckled Eternity's seatbelt, and picked her up in his arms. The way she hugged him and cried broke my heart. Tabari carried me inside, as I cried not only for my Eternity, but for Dove. I was starting to feel like this was my fault. I'm losing people I love, and putting loved ones in danger. I truly wish I never met that motherfucker! I just wanted this nightmare to end, and have my normal life back. Is that too much to ask for?

SIX

Tabari

I was so fucking mad that shit popped off the way it did. I literally, had that motherfucker exactly where I wanted him, and dropped the ball. The last person I expected to be there was A'miracle, and there was no way I was going to fuck around and harm her trying to kill Lazer's bitch ass. I couldn't front, I was pissed, because A'miracle should have told me where she was going. All I wanted to do was protect her, and things could have been avoided if she would have communicated with me. I texted her. She knows I texted her, and she didn't bother to reply, which threw me off.

"Man, how the fuck shorty get there? I know y'all not pulling stunts like this in front of bitches now? Come on, fam, you work smarter than that," Keahi stated, as I sat in the bathroom cleaning my arm. I was grazed by a bullet, nothing major, and I already hit up Choppa to make sure he and his team were good.

"Nah, I don't know what happened, fam. I literally, had the motherfucker, and was about to off his ass, until I saw A'miracle standing there. The crazy part is, the motherfucker was coming for them," I spoke, feeling my pressure rise even more.

"Yea, his ass asking for it. Shorty so fucked up, I don't even

44

know what to do," Keahi stated, referring to Eternity. I knew this had to be hard on both of them, since they watched their friend die like that. Shaking my head, I made sure the bandage was secure on my arm, before walking out of the bathroom and turning on the TV. I knew this shit would be all over the news, and I prayed none of our faces popped up. Keahi and I watched the news, trying to catch up on the story before there was a knock at the door. I opened it, and it was A'miracle. As bad as I wanted to be mad at her, I couldn't. Grabbing her, I pulled her into my arms and just held her. She was still shaking, and I knew she would be traumatized from this shit.

"Aye, I'm about to go check on shorty. I might crash here tonight, fam, to make sure Eternity good," Keahi stated, as he walked out of the room and left me and A'miracle alone. The news was still developing information on the story, and I quickly turned the TV off. I didn't want A'miracle to see this right now.

"Come mere', man," I stated, sitting on the bed. A'miracle walked over, and I pulled her on top of me. I laid back, as she straddled me and just looked at her. She kept wiping her eyes, trying to get herself together, and I gave her a moment. I needed her to understand exactly what I was about to say.

"I texted you," I said, seriously, looking her in her eyes.

"I know, I'm sorry," she replied.

"A'miracle,"

"No, it's my fault. I should have responded, and told you where I was. I shouldn't have went, to begin with. I should have stayed here, and eaten my food as I planned, but," she said, as she looked away from me.

"Now, my friend is dead. It's my fault," she whispered. I pulled her face closer to mine and kissed her lips. I hated for her to feel this way, and I needed her to know it wasn't her fault.

"It's not your fault, A'miracle. If I would have known you where there, none of the shit would have popped off as it did. The last thing I need is to scare you away from me, but you do need to know I will do everything in my power to protect you," I said, honestly, reaching up and wiping her tears away.

"I don't know what Dove wanted to tell me, and now, I never will. That's why I was there. After she and Eternity had words, she tried to run away, and we both ran after her. Maybe if I had just let her go, she would still be here. It's like, Lazer got excited when he saw us together. Like he had plans to hurt us both," A'miracle cried, causing me to bit the inside of my jaw. I hated to see her cry. Shit like this ate at my heart, and made me wanna kill Lazer again, even more.

"That motherfucker is getting everything coming his way. I can promise you that," I blurted, meaning every word of it.

"No, don't! I don't want to lose you. If that's my fate, then-"

"A'miracle, I'mma stop you right there, before you say some dumbass shit," I blurted, in a tone so stern, I knew I scared her.

"It's not your fate! That motherfucker killed my uncle! Lazer's ass threatened you, or have you forgotten?" I asked, looking at her as she shook her head no.

"There is no way in hell I'm going to let that motherfucker continue to walk this Earth, knowing that he took my uncle's life, and threatened my girl. I can promise you a lot of things, baby, and I'm good with promises. I will never break them when it comes to you. But please don't make me promise you that. I don't wanna disappoint you," I said, sitting up and kissing her lips again.

"From now on, you tell me your whereabouts. Matter of fact, where your phone?" I said, in a stern tone.

"It's downstairs, in my purse," she stated.

"Go get it," I demanded, sitting up and helping her off me. She quickly disappeared from my room. I used this time to start her a bath, because I knew she would need to relax. I had some aromatherapy bubble bath, I lit some aromatherapy candles too. Right now, it wasn't about sex, I just needed her to relax, so she could at least sleep at some point tonight. Watching someone get killed in front of your eyes is hard, especially if you don't live that life. A'miracle was a good girl, and she wasn't into the streets like this. It would probably be a little bearable if it was a random woman, but since it was her friend, I knew she would take this shit hard. Once I lit the candles, I walked back into my bedroom just as

46

she came in. She handed me her phone without any questions. I quickly shared her location with me, so that I could know where she was at all times. I wanted her to trust me, and know that I had her best interest at heart, and protection. All I wanted was to keep her safe, and I will use my last breath to do so.

"I'm running you a bath, because it's more that I wanna talk to you about. I need you to be open-minded to this discussion, and know that I only want the best for you. You understand?" I question. Again, she nodded her head. As the tub filled up, I held her in my arms. I calmly went over everything that I wanted to discuss with her in my head, while I helped her undress. Grabbing her hand, I led her to the tub, and helped her inside. I watched as she leaned her head back and closed her eyes. I let her have a moment before I spoke to her.

"A'miracle, I need you to trust me. I'm going to fix everything. I don't want you to worry about the police, or anything like that. Tonight, you didn't go to the club. Tonight, you stayed home, and Eternity came over. Y'all watched movies and ate food. Do you understand what I'm saying?" I asked, looking down at her. I was sitting on the edge of the tub, admiring how beautiful this girl truly was. I brushed her hair from her face before she opened her eyes and answered me.

"Yes, I understand," she responded.

"Anything in that club that may have your picture on it, I will have by morning. Everything will be erased, so you don't have to worry about that; including the little code that was scanned on your phone," I said, taking a deep breath, before bringing up a subject that I knew would hurt.

"Dove, does she have any relatives besides Wade? This will hit the news by morning, and they won't release her name to the public, before a family member identifies her body," I said, watching the tears roll down her face. She quickly wiped them away, as if she was trying to prove a point to me. As if she was trying to show me, she was strong, but I knew she was breaking apart inside.

"No, she doesn't. I mean, her mother left them when they were younger. Supposedly moved away with her boyfriend, leaving them to fend for themselves. Wade paid for her to go to school. I met him at an award ceremony. She doesn't have anyone to identify her body, but me or Eternity, if they allow us to. But I can't do that. I can't see her like that," A'miracle said to me, dabbing the tears away. Her eyes were so red and puffy, and I felt bad for bringing it up.

"I want you to go to therapy. Not only for the domestic stuff, but to really sit down and talk to a trained professional. A'miracle, everything that you have experienced is a lot to take on. If you not already secretly battling depression, then you will be. You might even suffer from PTSD, because of all of this shit! I hate that you're going through this, and I wish I could take the pain away. I just need you to know that I will be here every step of the way, and I will never leave your side. I will do my part as your man, but I need you to do your part as my woman. I need you to start your journey to healing, beautiful, you need to go to therapy. I'll go with you if they allow me to, and if they don't, I'll be waiting for you outside the door when you're done. I know this is easier said than done, but you can't bring up tonight again. You can't talk about it with anyone, including your therapist. You can mention seeing a loved one die, but nothing more. I got you, baby girl, I got us," I said, kissing her lips.

"I'm fine. I will be ok. I have so much work to do, in regards to getting my company back up and running. I can't let-"

"Don't worry about your company, I'll handle that. Don't worry about finding a building, I'll handle that too. I got you. All I'm asking is for you to go to therapy. Take some time to get yourself together, then make the appointments. Leave everything else up to me, ok?" I asked, gently rubbing the side of her face.

"Ok, Tabari, I'll go," A'miracle said, but that wasn't good enough for me.

"Promise me?" I asked, looking her in her eyes. She hesitated for a moment, before she nodded her head.

"I promise," and that was all I needed from her. I knew she had a hell of a road ahead, and I promised that I would be there. I don't make a promise that I can't keep. I needed A'miracle as much as she needed me...

SEVEN

A'miracle

----

*I*t's been a week, and I finally got myself out of bed. I doubted if I could do this, and wondered why I agreed to it. My body stood motionless, as I made sure the numbers on the glass door matched the address on Google. I wanted so badly to go back to my car, cry, and drive away, but I knew I couldn't break my promise to Tabari. He's literally, been by my side through all of this. I haven't been eating as much as I should, and I was so tired of not fully sleeping. Whenever I did, the nightmares were too much bear. I was losing myself, if I hadn't already done. Now, I was here at therapy, hoping this was the first step to getting myself back to normal. I looked at my car, contemplating getting in and driving off. I guess Tabari could feel I was having second thoughts since he texted me.

Tabari: *Strength doesn't come from the things you can do, but overcoming the things you can't. I believe in you and I know this is extremely difficult, but you can do this baby.*

I smiled at the message, since it gave me the little courage and extra push I needed to go inside. I stopped at the front desk to check in. I had to fill out some forms that asked pretty personal questions. I answered them to the best of my ability, and waited for the lady to escort me to the room. As we walked down the hall, I could hear chatter. It threw me off a bit, since I wasn't sure what to expect.

"A'miracle, you can find a seat anywhere you would like, and the class will begin shortly," the small woman said to me, with a smile. I forced myself to return one as I walked over to the closest seat I could get to. It was about six women here, talking amongst themselves, and I was having second thoughts about this since it was group therapy. I wasn't sure how a bunch of women could help me, when we're all in the same position. But if this was where I had to start, the least I could do is give it a fair shot.

"Hi, I'm Paige. Is it your first time here?" Another woman asked, taking a seat next to me. She was a chubby woman, and very pretty. Her skin was hazelnut brown, and glowed liked Gabrielle Union. Her hair was pulled back into a ponytail, and she had the prettiest light brown eye. The other one was covered with an eye patch, but it still didn't take away from how beautiful she looked.

"Hi, Paige, I'm A'miracle. It's nice to meet you," I responded, finally stopping staring at the woman, and shaking her hand. I felt bad, and hoped I didn't offend her with my staring.

"It's my first time here. I don't know if this is for me," I said, honestly, looking around at the other women. They all looked polite and friendly, but I just didn't think I was ready for this yet.

"It's perfectly fine to feel like this, A'miracle. Just know we're a family, and we don't judge. We're here to help one another. You never know, your story could be the message to save someone's life. My life was saved through this program. I lost an eye, but that's better than losing my heartbeat," Paige said, as the doors opened. I turned around to find two women walking towards the group. I'm assuming this had to be the therapist, since all of the women who were standing around in a huddle quickly found their seats. I could see that one of the women appeared to be distraught. I mean, she was crying her eyes out, and I wondered what was wrong.

"Healing doesn't mean the damage never exists. It means?" The woman asked, looking out into the group.

"It no longer controls our lives," everyone responded, in unison.

"Today is a hard topic for us. We're discussion forgiveness," the therapist said, looking at me. She stared at me for a while, which made me feel a little uncomfortable. It's was weird, but her smile was warming.

"I see new faces. Thank you for joining us. I'm Zofiaa," the therapist nodded towards me. I didn't know why, but I just felt the need to introduce myself to her, so I stood up.

"I'm A'miracle. Thank you for having me," I said, looking at the woman. Her skin was flawless, and makeup was on point. As I looked around the room, I realized there were special details about each woman in this class. They all had some sort of war wounds, which made me admire each and every one of them.

"Nice to meet you, A'miracle. We'll set up one on one's later, just to get to know you. Don't worry, I do this with everyone to get to know them better," Zofiaa said, making me feel a little comfortable. Maybe coming to this class wasn't so bad after all. I took my seat and waited for Zofiaa to continue.

"Forgiveness is hard. It doesn't happen overnight, but when you forgive, you choose to live. Those who have hurt you, live rent-free in your head. Day in, and day out, that's all you think about is them, and how they have hurt you in some way. How is that fair? Especially when they sleep well at night, and you don't. You have to forgive," Zofiaa said, making perfectly good sense, but I wasn't sure if I was ready for that. I know I needed to forgive Wade, but he truly broke me. Yes, the fight was extremely bad, and I will never heal from that but, he also attempted to ruin me; my career. These past few weeks have been hard. It seems like I'll never get a break, and every bad thing that occurs, links back to Wade in some way. The last thing I wanted to do was lose someone I love because of him, and I did. It was his blood sister, which makes things even worse.

"Dominique wants to share her story today, as well as some extremely bad news. We must pray for each other, and continue to be each other's strength. If you feel as if you're not loved in your everyday life, and relationships, then let me be the first to tell you that you are loved. You are loved here," Zofiaa kindheartedly expressed, pulling Dominique in for another embrace. Dominique used the tissues she was holding and wiped away her tears, trying to gather herself. I hated being the emotional type, where if someone is crying, I find myself on the verge of tears as well.

"Forgiveness is something that I seek daily. Not only have I been a victim, but I've also been the villain," Dominique stated, looking up at the ceiling. I could tell that the story she was sharing was extremely hard for her. Although I didn't personally know the woman, my heart went out to her.

"I've done so many things in my life that I regret, and I kinda thought getting my ass whooped on a daily was my karma. So, I felt like this was God's way of punishing me," Dominique shrugged, continuing her story.

"I didn't have anything, no family, no place to go, so I couldn't leave him. I thought he really loved me, and although his actions showed differently, I still stayed. Even when I almost slipped into a coma because of him, I still couldn't leave him," Dominique fearfully shared, wiping away more tears. By now, everyone in the room was crying. The connection they all shared was something I could be apart of. No one was judging, and she had everyone's undivided attention.

"I did the ultimate, and that's put a man before my children. I mean, I carried them both for nine months, and put a man I barely knew before them. What type of mother, what type of real mother does this? For so long, I wondered about my babies, and how they were doing without me. Whenever I was depressed about them, I got beat. Whenever I mentioned their names, I got beat. If I told anyone I was a mother, I got beat. I was so stupid in love that I walked out on my children when they needed me the most, for someone who attempted to kill me multiple times," Dominique explained. Just listening to the things she went through in her relationship was heartbreaking.

"That man beat me for everything, and yet, I still stayed. He would have literally, been the death of me, if he didn't go first. He died from an overdose, and that was the happiest day of my life," Dominique said looking out at us. Her story was touching, and I could feel the tears falling from my eyes.

"When he died, I took that as my opportunity to take my life back. I was now in control. I got myself clean, which was hard work, but I did it. I found a wonderful family here with you guys, but it was something that was always missing," Dominique stated, as she looked at the therapist.

"Go ahead, Dominique. Remember, this is the first step to healing," Zofiaa responded.

"I've always wondered where my babies were, and if my children were ok. I looked for them when I got myself together, but was afraid to reach out. When I got the courage, I reached out to my son, but he didn't want anything to do with me. Now, I think I've wasted time that I can't get back," Dominique said, pulling a picture from her jacket. Her hands shook as she looked at the photograph and continued to cry. I wonder what it was a picture of that hurt her so bad.

"I don't blame my son, and I know he hates me. But my daughter, my beautiful baby girl," Dominique cried, pointing to the ceiling. Instantly, sighs were heard throughout the room, and everyone was in tears, yet again.

"She's dead, she was murdered, and as a mother, I wasn't there to protect her. I wasn't there to teach her how she's supposed to be loved. I wasn't there to explaining anything to her that she needed to know as a woman. Now, all I have left are memories and this picture," Dominique cried, holding it up.

"Do you mind if they see the beautiful family you have?" Zofiaa asked Dominique, as she looked at the picture. She nodded her head and handed the picture to one of the women in the front row. One by one they all looked at the picture and passed it around, as Dominique continued her story. When the picture got in my hands, I damn near screamed. I couldn't believe what I was holding. My hands started shaking and my chest heaved up and down. Dove and Wade looked so young in this picture, but there was no denying it was them.

They looked like siblings should; like they loved each other. Dove's arms wrapped around Wade's neck, and they both had the brightest smiles. Here I am mourning the loss of one of my closest friends, and now I'm in therapy with her mother! I became sick to my stomach as I passed the picture to the woman next to me, and ran out of the door. I couldn't even make it to the bathroom before I released the contents of my stomach in the trash can.

Once I calmed myself, I turned around, and found Zofiaa standing next to me. I was crying so bad, that she wrapped her arms around me for comfort. I couldn't believe Dove's mother was here. She found out Dove was dead, and I wasn't worried that she knew who I was, since they didn't have a relationship. She didn't see her kids grow up. I think I made myself sick with the thought of knowing who she was, and she had no clue who I was. Dove always wanted a relationship with her mother, and promised herself that she would look for her one day, and now she will never get that chance. The pain in my heart stung. It felt like I could literally, feel the strings of my heart tearing apart.

"A'miracle, are you ok, sweetie?" Zofiaa asked, finally letting me go.

"Yes, I'm sorry. I can't do this. Thank you," I said, quickly trying to gather myself and walk away from her.

"Wait," Zofiaa said calling out to me, but I ignored her and continued to walk towards the door, until she stopped me.

"A'miracle, you were brought here for a reason, don't give up so soon. If group therapy is too much for you right now, then we can do one on one on your terms. I'm here to help you, and something is telling me you need me. We can meet up wherever you want, Starbucks, Deli, anywhere," she said, looking me in my eyes. Her suggestions sounded good, but I really didn't think I could do this. Maybe this wasn't for me, or maybe it was too soon.

"Listen, take my card and call me. We can set something up for later this week, but please, A'miracle, give therapy a chance. I'm here to help you," Zofiaa smiled, before walking away and leaving me to my thoughts. I put her card in my purse and walked to my car. Once inside, I called Tabari. I couldn't even get the words out, since he already knew something was wrong. The only thing I wanted was him. The only thing he said was, "come home," and I did just that...

EIGHT

Tabari

I demanded A'miracle to close her eyes the moment she stepped foot inside the house. I told her to relax, and that the outside world no longer existed while she was in my presence. I could tell from the look on her face, and the smile that graced her lips, that she had no idea what I was up too. I could see the excitement, yet uneasiness, she held, and knew her day didn't go as planned, but it was about to get ten times better. Hell, I was proud that she took the first step, and even more amazed that she kept her word; she kept her promise. For that, she deserved a reward.

Seeking therapy in the black community isn't talked about. In fact, you'll find yourself being talked about if you seek help. People mistake depression and anxiety as being sad and anxious, and it's way deeper than that. Depression isn't something that should be taken lightly. So many women, so many black women, suffer in silence. Since society has brainwashed the world to acknowledge black women as being strong and independent, being broken is unheard of. This is very true, since I believe all black women are strong, independent, and beautiful. That doesn't mean the most precious gift God has blessed the Earth with, doesn't get tired of being Superwoman.

I get it, and I needed A'miracle to know that I get it. I needed her to know that she doesn't have to be Superwoman anymore, and that her Superman was here. I knew she had been crying from the conversation we had prior, which only made me want her home more. Grabbing her hand, I led her upstairs, and let her hand go, once we made it to the top. I pointed in the direction I wanted her to walk in, as she smiled and followed the trail of red rose petals. The entire day that she was out, I decided to do something special for her. I wanted to take the stress away, and see that gorgeous smile of hers. When she entered the bedroom, I heard her gasp, right before she placed her hands over her mouth. The reaction I was expecting was happening right before my eyes, and I loved every bit of it. I had to laugh to myself since I didn't think I would pull it off. I had rose petals everywhere, and a 90's R&B playlist playing in the background. The teacup candles led from the entrance of the bedroom door, to the bathroom, then over to the bed. Next to the bed was a bottle of Rose champagne on ice, and two champagne flutes. I already had her bath water ran, and was simply waiting for her to come home. Candles were lit all over the room, silk white sheets were fresh on the bed, and all I wanted was to cater to her. I wanted to show my appreciation to her, to the woman I was slowly falling for.

"You like my surprise?" I asked, walking up behind her. I kissed the nape of her neck, and could smell the sweet scent of her perfume.

"I love it, Tabari," she replied, as I guided her to the bathroom. Piece, by piece, I removed her clothes. I literally, didn't want her to move one finger. She's done enough for a lifetime, and it's time for her to experience the benefits of fucking with a real man. I wanted to cater to her, make love to her, make her body cum more ways than she could count. Once she was undressed, I helped her inside of the warm bath. A slight moan escaped her lips the moment the warm water kissed her skin. She leaned her head back, and I was waiting for that one moment. That one thing that I wanted her to do, and she finally did; she exhaled.

"This feels so good," she expressed, barely above a whisper. I looked at A'miracle in her barest state. I stared at this woman like I've never stared at any other woman before. This was surreal to me, since I didn't think I'd get another shot a love. Not me, not in this lifetime, but God has a way of showing up and showing out. Reaching my hand inside the water, I began to wash her body with her favorite scented Dove. The entire time, her eyes never left me, as I slowly washed every inch of her. The bath was just warming her up for everything else I had I stored for the night.

"Is the temperature of the water ok?" I whispered, looking up at her. Her smile never left her lips as she nodded her head yes.

"Baby, you can use words," I joked, smirking at her.

"I know, I'm just speechless. No one has done anything like this for me before," she explained, closing her eyes. After washing her up, I held her hand for a while, and let her soak. I let her thoughts roam, as well as mine. I didn't want to say anything, just admire the beauty before me. The art of intimacy is more than just sex. Most men feel as if intimacy and sex are one and the same, but I felt completely different. Intimacy is more than two bodies connecting together, but two minds. It's knowing your partner's needs and wants, before they even grace their lips. It's connecting on a level where neither one of you need to say anything, but in silence, you both speak volumes in any room. It's being emotionally, and mentally connected, before physical. Attraction comes easy, but what I want has to be built. I wanted a solid foundation that eventually leads to love. I seek happiness more these days over anything. Sex comes and goes, but love, love stays.

Before getting up, I stole a kiss, and walked out of the room and down to the kitchen. I grabbed the platter out of the fridge, and was heading back upstairs, until I saw a shadow at my front door. Fucking with Choppa and his thug ass ways were rubbing off on me. I quickly put the platter on the couch, and grabbed the gun that was underneath the cushion. Not wanting to wait for a mother-fucker to murk me first, I swung the front door opened with my gun pointed directly at the person before me. I damn nearer pulled the trigger when I saw who it was.

"Fuck are you doing here?" I questioned, looking at Brianna's dumbass. I could see her stomach as she put her hands up. She was very much pregnant, but it wasn't mine.

"Please, don't shoot," Brianna said, looking around.

"I've been calling you," she spat, shifting her weight from one foot to the next. I tucked my gun in the back of my pants before responding to her.

"You're blocked, Brianna. Stop calling my fucking mama's house too, playing on the phone and shit. A nigga ain't got time for all the games you play, and we been done. I'm not sure what part of that don't you understand. I wish you nothing but the best, but don't pop up at my crib any more. I almost shot your stupid ass," I said, attempting to close the door in her face, but she stuck her foot inside, which pissed me off even more. Looking down at it, I wanted to push her ass, but the last thing I needed was her to hurt herself, or the child she was carrying, on my doorstep.

"Brianna?" I stated, in a calm, yet venomous tone, which led her to move her foot.

"Look, just hear me out, Tabari, please. I know you. You want kids, that's what you've always wanted. Now, we're about to have one and you're ignoring me? Is that how you're supposed to treat the mother of your child?" Brianna asked, with her voice getting louder by the second. It caused me to step outside, since I didn't wanna make a scene, or risk A'miracle seeing or hearing her. I needed to get up close in personal with this bitch to get my message across. I stepped so closly to her face, that I could tell her ass the last thing she'd eaten. I could tell she was nervous, and wasn't sure what I was going to do.

"Look, Brianna, you and I both know that fucking baby ain't mine. I haven't touched you in months, and when I did, I always strapped up. You not about to pull a fast one on me, cause I'm not a dumbass nigga. Don't try to play me like a fool. I'm not the fucking one to play with. Now, I've asked you nicely. If I have to repeat myself, you not going to like it, Brianna. Now get the fuck off my porch," I said, walking back inside. She just stood there waiting for me to say something, but instead, I closed the door in her face.

"Crazy bitch," I mumbled under my breath, putting the gun

back underneath the cushion. I fucked up one day letting this bitch slide through. I usually don't bring bitches to where I lay my head at, unless I was truly fucking with them. Brianna's ass was a thot, and the bitch ain't been right since I ran up in her. Hopefully, she got the message this time. Picking up the tray, I went back upstairs. A'miracle's eyes were still closed when I walked back inside the bathroom. I placed the tray on the sink before sitting on the edge of the tub.

"Baby, keep your eyes closed, ok?" I asked, covering them for her. I laughed, since I knew she would open them first.

"Wait, what are you doing?" She asked.

"You just don't listen, huh? I feel your eyelashes moving," I laughed, causing her to laugh with me.

"Keep your eyes closed. You trust me, right?" I asked, already knowing the answer.

"Yes, I do," she replied, as I kissed her lips again.

"Tell me how this taste," I said, picking up a strawberry and bringing it to her lips. I circled her lips with the fruit, before telling her to take a bite.

"It's good. Strawberries are my favorite," A'miracle said, as I replaced it with a grape. For the next ten minutes or so, I fed her fruits, while she relaxed in a bubble bath. After I was done, I helped her out of the tub, and proceeded to dry her off. Leading her back to the bed, I told her to lay on her stomach.

"Wait, you don't want me to put on clothes?" She asked, causing me to laugh at her.

"If I wanted you in clothes, then I would have put them on you. Stop asking so many questions, woman, and let ya' man take care of you," I stated, hoping she caught on to what I was saying. After everything we've been through together, there was no way I was letting this woman go. I know she said that she didn't really want to jump headfirst back into a relationship, but I didn't believe it. I knew she was feeling me, just as bad as I was feeling her. I just prayed that Wade hadn't scared her into believing that all men are the same. I would work overtime to prove that I'm not him. Just prayed she was up for the ride.

I took off my shirt, as the playlist switched to *Bobby V Ft. K. Michelle- Put It In.* Lord knows that exactly what I wanted to do, from looking at how fat her ass sct up. Damn, A'miracle had the perfect body. All her shit was real. She wasn't sucked or plucked or any of the new shit women are doing now. Don't get me wrong, I'm not knocking it, a man like me just loves homegrown shit. I eased my way on the bed, and grabbed the sensual oil out of the warmer it was in. I poured a little into my hands, before starting at the bottom and working my way to the top.

"Ohh, that feels good," A'miracle moaned, as I massaged her calf's first. I focused on the areas I knew would relax her most. She's been doing a lot of running around, so I'm sure not only her feet, but her calf's needed some attention. The lemongrass scent filled the room as I massaged deep into her muscles. The sounds she was making was not only building my head up, but making my dick hard.

As I worked my way down to her feet, I couldn't help but admire how pretty they were. They looked freshly polished, even if they weren't, and the color was a light green. I kissed her feet gently, before sucking her toes.

"Oooh, Tabari," A'miracle moaned out. I placed each of them in my mouth one by one making sure to give them all attention. I had her legs shaking already, and I haven't even begun to eat her pussy. Tonight, was all about her. I just wanted to make her feel good in every way I possibly could. I poured the warm oil all over her back before I massaged it. I focused on the lower areas more, just to be close to her fat ass. Before I knew it, my tongue trailed the spine of her back, before biting and kissing both of her ass cheeks. Spreading them apart gently, I buried my face in between them, eating her pussy and ass at the same damn time.

"Oooh, fuck!" A'miracle yelled out, as I sucked her clit the way she liked it. It only took me one time to eat your pussy to know exactly what to do to make you cum in less than ninety seconds. She was almost there, but I didn't want her to cum this way.

"Sit on my face," I demanded, slapping her ass. I laid down in the middle of the bed and helped her. The moment her sweet scent hit my nostrils, I ate her pussy like I'd haven't eaten in days. I guided her waist back and forth, instructing her on how to ride my face. With one of my free hands, I squeezed her breasts and pinched her nipples. I slapped her ass each time she rolled her pussy in my face, letting her know I was enjoying every moment. The more she moaned, the moaned the more excited I became. I could feel the pre-cum oozing out of my dick.

"I'm cumming!" She screamed out to me, as her entire body shook. She came so hard that the nut was dripping down the side of my face, and into my ears. Without warning, I pushed her backward, and grabbed the condom that was already on the dresser. Once I slid it on, I eased my dick inside her warmth, before fucking her as if her ex nigga lived in the apartment below us. The only thing that could be heard was her screams, my grunts, and the wetness we both shared. I pinned her legs above her head, and fucked her and played with her pussy until she came once again. This time, I came right along with her. Once I cleaned us both up, I laid next to her before pulling her directly on top of me. I held her close, as light snores escaped. I kissed her forehead a million times, and simply watched her sleep...

NINE

A'miracle

$\mathcal{I}$ stayed in the bed majority of the day, since Tabari wore my ass out. Last night was every bit of amazing. He was so damn sweet and sincere. I knew that everything he's done for me has come straight from his heart. It really made me wonder why he isn't married, and why hasn't a woman scooped him up yet. I'd have to ask him about that, since we haven't talked about his relationships. Crazy he knows mine and I never asked about his. Hopefully, he didn't take that as me not caring, because I did. Honestly, it just slipped my mind, I guess.

I didn't wanna do anything today but sleep and watch Netflix's, but I couldn't get my mind off this box. I had already called Eternity to check up on her, and to my surprise, she wasn't in bed alone. Come to find out, her and Keahi had been kicking it hella hard lately. It was good to see her smiling and laughing again, and finally dating. She was so anti-men and being independent that I thought she would never give love a try again. I hated that we both had to experience something so traumatizing, but it was good to know we were on the right track to getting our lives back in order. Dove's family had a private funeral. We didn't find out about it until someone posted the obituary. I was heartbroken, since we didn't get to say our final goodbyes, but Eternity and I planned to go put flowers down for her soon.

Getting out of bed, I walked over to the box that was sitting on the floor by the dresser. I said a silent prayer to myself before I opened it. Inside was a small plastic bottle, two diapers, and a blanket. The diapers looked like it had stains on it, but it was too old to tell. None of this could help me, so why did she keep it? Sighing, I put all of the contents back in the box, and put it on the floor. I could feel myself getting a headache just trying to put the pieces together.

Since I brought my computer to Tabari's house, I decided to do some work. I know he said he would handle everything, but I was never the type to put all of my eggs in one basket. Just because things were a little out of order, didn't mean I would hide under a rock. I had a company to run, business to take care of, and money to make. My assistant, Nicole, was so damn helpful. She had been doing follow up's on all of my clients, and checking in on the projects, without me even having to ask. To my surprise, business actually went up seven percent. I thought with the loss of my building, and the fact that I didn't physically have a place to meet my clients, that my company was doomed. Nicole had been planning and meeting with clients, and sending over contracts for me. I swear, this girl was going to get the biggest raise as soon as I get things back in order.

Most of the jobs were done, except for Mr. Martinez. This fucking man was driving me crazy. First, he cursed me out, then sent a threatening email. Instead of responding to his ass, I simply took a picture of the shit, and sent it to Tabari. What's the point of arguing with a man, when I have a man to do it for me? Damn, I have a man. That felt so good to say. I know at first, I didn't wanna date, in fear of being mistreated again, but there was no way in hell I was letting this good man go. He has literally, gone out of his way daily to keep a smile on my face. It's like I knew he had a business to run of his own, but damn, I missed him when we were apart. Looking at my phone, I quickly sent him an I miss you text before I got a text of my own. It was my mother, telling me to get to the hospital, and that something was wrong with my father.

My heart cringed just from the thought of losing him. I felt so stupid for allowing Wade to come between our relationship, and I will never forgive myself for it. Once I showered, I grabbed my keys, locked everything up, and went straight to the hospital. I knew Tabari said he wanted to know my every move, so I made Siri send him a text. I was too shook up to call, or text him, anything at this point. I just needed to focus my attention on the road and getting to my father as quick and as safely as possible. It felt like I made it to the hospital in record-breaking time. I knew I was about to have tickets up the ass, since I was running lights trying to get here. I tried to stay on side streets as much as possible to avoid the police. When I got off the elevator on my father's floor, my mother was standing outside his door pacing. I was afraid to ask what was wrong, afraid to even walk in her direction. But the moment she saw me, she ran into my arms.

"Mom, is he, is he-"

"No, baby, he's not. He just having complications," my mother said, wiping her tears away and mine. I couldn't even get the word out of my mouth. I couldn't say dead, and my father's name in the same sentence; I just couldn't.

"He needs a transplant now, or we will lose him, A'miracle. His kidneys are failing, the doctors aren't sure how much longer his body can put up a fight," my mother said, causing me to gasp. I couldn't imagine losing my father, and I prayed that a miracle happened. I wish it was something I could do, someone I could call. But I knew I couldn't do anything but pray. The doctors came out and said that my father was doing ok for now. They had to put a tube down his throat to help him breathe, and that he's heavily medicated. When I walked inside, I instantly started crying harder. Who wants to see one of their parents like this? Your parents are who you go to when something isn't right. They help you get better when you're sick. Now, since the tables have turned, I felt so damn useless. My father really needed me, and it was nothing I could do.

Although he was still alive, he looked terrible. It seemed to be more tubes than last time, and he was laying flat on his back. I held his hand, begging for him to squeeze mine back. I kissed his cheek, hoping he would feel me, and open his eyes a little. He wasn't in a coma or anything, just pretty doped up. I didn't know how much more my father's body could take, and this was really taking a toll on me. I wasn't ready to say goodbye.

"Daddy, I love you so much, and I'm so sorry. Please forgive me. I promise when you make it through this, we will rebuild our relationship. We can start all the way over if you like. You're my Superman, and I can't lose you. You're the strongest man I know, and I know you won't let this beat you. Please keep fighting, Daddy," I cried, kissing his cheek. Before I knew it, I was in the hallway, demanding to speak with his doctor. I knew how hospitals worked, or at least, I thought I did. The more money you have, the better chance you have at living. My father's name is on the transplant list, and his doctors needed to be working overtime to get him a kidney. I didn't give a fuck about protocol, or if someone's name was before his. I needed my father to live; I needed my daddy.

"Dr. Kirby, I'm upset, and I apologize for the way I'm acting, but there has to be something you can do?" I spat, pacing the floor of his office. My mind and emotions were all over the place. After I cursed out damn near the entire staff on my father's floor, Dr. Kirby was called. Instead of allowing the security to escort me from the building, Dr. Kirby took me to his office.

"Ms. Evans, I understand your frustration, and I can only imagine how difficult this time may be for you. I'm doing the best that I can to ensure that your father is comfortable, and that-"

"See, that's the thing, I don't need him to be comfortable. I need him to live! I need you to do your best, and make sure he stays alive!" I shouted, looking at him like he was crazy.

"The only thing we can do is wait. That's it. When a kidney becomes available, we will be contacted if it's a match. When I know something, I will inform you, I promise, A'miracle. You have my word," Dr. Kirby said, sincerely.

"In the meantime, please be nice to my staff. They're doing the best they can for your father. Speaking of which, I'm sorry about the incident that occurred. That was not the way I, or my staff, should have handled that situation," Dr. Kirby stated.

"The situation about me being twenty-six years old and finding out I'm adopted? It's fine. It's more to it than just the obvious," I said, looking down at the floor. The more I talked about it, the better I felt. I knew the back story now, so I wasn't upset like I was before. But none of that mattered. I just wanted my father to live.

"A'miracle, I usually don't do this, and I could get in a boatload of trouble, for even suggesting this," Dr. Kirby hesitated, looking at me, then down at the forms in front of him.

"I know a few, higher up. I can pull some strings, and you can go down and get some test ran in the DNA database," he suggested, which confused the hell out of me.

"Test for what? Isn't that used for like criminals and stuff like that?" I asked.

"To find your biological parents, A'miracle, and you're right. That is how the database is running, but on the brighter side, it's one of the biggest in the world. If your parents have done anything, their DNA is there. I mean, only if you want to, because I know this sounds weird," Dr. Kirby stated.

"Yes, it really does, but you have my attention," I explained, finally taking a seat.

"With the new technology, they can test you, and run your information through the database. If somehow, there's a match they will contact you. It's pretty simple," he said, like people did this normally. Here I was thinking I would have to contact Maury, and see if he could get down to the bottom of this.

"Yea, as weird as that sounds, I'm willing to try just about anything to get the answers I need. What's the next step?" I asked, looking at my phone. Tabari finally texted me back, so I quickly responded to let him know what was going on.

"Here, take this. The address is at the bottom. I'll call and let them know you're on your way over. The only thing I need you to do is keep our little mistake between us. I could lose-"

"I know. I said it's fine. I won't sue, or contact HIPPA. You have my word," I said, looking at him, then down at the paper in my hand. Was I really ready to do this? Can I handle the information I was attempting to find? I thanked Dr. Kirby for the information he gave me, before going back up to my father's room. I kissed his cheek, and my mother's, before I left. I needed to get some fresh air. I couldn't stand seeing him like that. It felt like he was literally, dying before my eyes, and there was nothing anyone could do.

I headed over to the address Dr. Kirby gave me. I thought the process would take longer, but after filling out forms, and getting my mouth swopped, I was done. The women told me that the results would be available on the site. The only thing I needed to do was log in with my username and password. There wasn't a time frame since it could take a while. She just told me to be on the lookout for an email with instructions. I thank her for her help and went back to my car. Looking at my phone, I wanted to call Tabari, but I didn't wanna stop him from handling his business. I needed to vent, to talk to someone who could understand what I was truly feeling. Sighing, I took a chance, and called the only person I knew who was trained for this. The phone rang a few times before she answered.

"Hey, Zofiaa. It's A'miracle. Umm, can we meet? Please, I just need to talk," I said, hoping she wasn't too busy. She agreed, and told me where to meet her. Moments later, I pulled my car out of the parking lot and headed in that direction. I was starting to feel like I was losing myself daily. If it wasn't one thing it was another...

I walked into Starbucks, and looked around, until I saw Zofiaa. She was seated in the back in a booth. Her smile was comforting, as I made my way over to the table. Instead of shaking her hand, she stood and gave me a hug. It's crazy, since it was needed. I know it's weird to hug complete strangers, but sometimes, a hug is all you need to make things better.

"I hope traffic wasn't too bad, and you found a close park," Zofiaa said, as we both slid into the booth. We were at a small and cozy Starbucks on Taylor Street, that I had no idea was here. I would definitely be back to get some work done.

"No, traffic wasn't that bad, I guess. I don't know wasn't really paying attention," I said, looking around. I was nervous, and I didn't know why. Then again, I did. I didn't want this woman to judge me, although I'm sure she wouldn't. I mean, isn't that against the rules of being a therapist? I wasn't sure how this worked, but here goes nothing.

"You seem like a lot is on your mind. How about I grab us some iced tea and we can talk? We can talk about whatever you want," Zofiaa stated, reaching her hand across the table to touch mine. I smiled at her, and appreciated the fact that she was going out of her way to make me feel comfortable.

"Sure, but I can pay," I offered, feeling like it's the least I could do.

"Nonsense, I got it," Zofiaa offered, as she got up from the booth.

"Passion Tango Tea Lemonade?" Zofiaa asked.

"I've never had it, but it sounds delicious," I smiled, as she walked away and towards the small line that developed. I took this time to calm my breathing. I felt warm all of a sudden, and I knew it had to be anxiety. Thankfully, I wore a short-sleeved shirt, I quickly slipped out of my jacket, hoping it would help. I already looked up symptoms on Google, and compared them to mine. The intense breathing, rapid heart rate, and sweating, were all caused by anxiety. I closed my eyes and counted backwards from 30, and took slow deep breaths. I placed my palms flat down on the table and pressed. I attempted to block everything out, and focused on something happy. Once I felt ok, I opened my eyes just in time as Zofiaa made it back to the table.

"I'm sure you're going to love it, so I got you a venti. This is one of my favorite teas here," Zofiaa smiled, as she placed the tea in front of me. I thanked her before taking a sip. It really was good. Usually, I get caramel frappes, but this will definitely be healthier.

"How did you get this?" Zofiaa asked, gently touching my arm. The scar wasn't as big as it used to be, but it was noticeable. I was about to say it was a birthmark, until I remembered what my mother, well, adopted mother, said.

"Honestly, I don't know. I thought I was born with it, but that changed in a matter of weeks," I said, shrugging and sitting back. I glanced out of the window, then caught Zofiaa just staring at me. It was awkward, but I brushed it off.

"Wanna talk about it?" Zofiaa asked, looking at me. There was no point in wasting this woman's time, so I may as well get everything off my chest. I took a deep breath, and told her everything; from the beginning to the end. When I was done, we had drunk two ice teas, ate salads, and snacked on cake pops. I knew my story was hard to bear, because I could see her tearing up as I explained everything to her. I mean, I cried too, and she comforted me through the tears, through the pain I relived, and I actually felt better afterward.

"Wow, girl, you've definitely been through a lot. I'm here to tell you things will get better. It's easier said than done, but it will get better. As far as your relationship with Wade, that was toxic. I'm glad you had the strength to get out when you did. For that, you should feel powerful, because you chose you. Staying and longer was allowing him to have control over you in every way. Most of us women don't have that power or strength. We tend to wait until the last minute, which ultimately ends with our lives being taken. That's really the ending result. I mean, there are programs you can get in, but they all don't work. You can move and change identities, but who wants to leave their life, their friends, and family? It's not fair. Then orders of protection is a waste of time. The police can't do anything until the person actually does something to you. By that time, women would end up dead. The laws really need to change when it comes to protecting women. With me and the programs and resources I have, I'm making a change. I'm proud of you, A'miracle," Zofiaa said, looking at me, making me cry even more. I can't lie and say that the thought of going back hasn't crossed my mind. It has, and I even wondered if he would get his shit together for me. If he would possibly go to counseling. Then, the images of him hitting me, raping me, and the pain I endured, all came back. If he did this once, he would surely do it again. Next time, I probably wouldn't be so lucky, and I couldn't gamble with my life like that. I love me, and I couldn't chance it. I couldn't roll the dice with my life in the palms of Wade's hands. No matter how much I loved him. No matter how much time I've invested, staying in something that could potentially kill me, is stupid.

"With your biological mother, I mean, parents, do you wanna find them? Is that something you truly want?" She asked, causing me to think long and hard. Did I really wanna find them? Would I be ok and accept everything that comes along with them?

"I don't know how to answer that question, Zofiaa. I mean, of course, I want to find my real parents. I have a lot of questions, you know? But I'm also scared," I revealed, honestly. I was terrified actually. What if I go looking for them, and they never wanted me too? What if I find something I'm not fully ready to accept? I mean, it's a lot to think about, to prepare for. Was this truly something I could handle? I'm a firm believer in when you go looking for something, you will find it.

"What if my mother doesn't want me to ever reach out and find her? What if she moved on and had other children? What if my dad was never in the picture to begin with? What if he never even knew I exist?" I asked Zofiaa, as if she could really answer these questions. The more I talked about it, the more frustrated I became. Maybe it was best that I didn't know. Maybe I should just forget looking for them, and be grateful for the parents I do have.

"I'm not trying to break up a happy home, I just want answers," I expressed, for the first time. It wasn't that I wanted to find my biological mother or parents, for rekindling. I honestly just wanted to know, why?

"You seem frustrated when you talk about your biological parents. Why?" Zofiaa asked, catching me off guard. Didn't she hear everything I just said? I guess it showed in my face, since she laughed before holding her hands up.

"Wow, calm down, A'miracle. I didn't mean it like that," Zofiaa said, reaching across the table and grabbing my hand. This time she held it which was different, but a good different.

"I'm not one of those therapists that tell you what you want to hear. I will ask you some tough questions, and get under your skin, and maybe on your nerves at times. But I need you to trust me, and believe in me. Believe in my process. I'm going to get you through this," Zofiaa said, reassuring me. I smiled, since she seemed like she sincerely cared. I wondered if she had children of her own. She seemed like she would be a great mother. Shaking the thoughts from my head, I finally answered her question.

"I'm frustrated, because I want to know why. What made me so terrible, so bad that my parents didn't want me? Like, what did I do as a baby, that made them not want me? Why carry me for nine months, only to leave me on the streets in a fucking box?" I spoke with so much anger, that I was starting to get a headache. I hadn't noticed I was crying, until I looked up and saw Zofiaa staring at me with a blank face. Her eyes filled with tears too, and I wondered why she was crying. She continued to look back and forth, from my arm to me, which was strange, but I didn't say anything.

"What if it was for good reasoning? I mean, I have to play devil's advocate, here. What if your mother, I mean, your parents, decided that was best at the time?" Zofiaa asked me, causing me to think of a scenario, a different approach to this situation.

"I never thought of it like that. I didn't think that maybe something could have been wrong, and maybe this was in my best interest," I said, looking at my phone light up. It was Tabari calling me, and I knew I had to leave. I wasn't expecting to be out this late, but it really did feel good to speak with her.

"Listen, I want you to do something for me. I want you to write a letter to your parents. Sit back and think about all the things you want to say to them. Things you want to share with them. No matter how long the letter is, no matter how much it makes you cry, write it. Get all of your feelings out; both good and bad. That's your assignment," Zofiaa said, squeezing my hand. She smiled at me, and I returned the gesture, just as Tabari called me again.

"I know you have to go, sweetie, please text me and let me know you made it home safe," Zofiaa said, standing. I did the same and slipped my jacket back on. After hugging once more and saying our goodbyes, I got in my car and called Tabari back. It felt like a weight was lifted from my shoulders talking to her. Although I knew this would be hard, and I had a long way to go, I had a better outlook on therapy. I told him I was on my way home, just needed to stop at Walgreens. I needed to grab a notebook and pens. I wanted to start on the letter the first thing in the morning.

TEN

Zofiaa

$\mathcal{I}$ was numb, completely in shock, as I sat on my couch, rocking back and forth. I knew God worked in mysterious ways, but this, He has really outdone himself this time. I've never seen anything so beautiful. She was a spitting image of everything I used to be, with a small shade of her father. Her conversation, her voice, the way she looked away when she was nervous, her smile, my God she was perfect. She was everything I was once upon a time. Everything about her was absolutely perfect. I know they say the apple doesn't fall far from the tree, and I was living proof of that. I wasn't sure if this was God's way of giving me a second chance, or just giving me back everything I've lost. Her pain, her tears, her late nights of wondering why, I would take all of it away, just to make sure she smiles for the rest of her life.

She was a blessing, she was my blessing. I still couldn't wrap my mind around the fact that this was truly happening, that this was real. Looking at the floor length mirror that was in my living room, I grabbed the package of makeup remover wipes from the table and sat in front of the mirror. I pulled my legs underneath me as I've always done. I removed my wig, revealing small, yet, thick braids. Some of my hair was missing in spots, and would never grow back from what I went through. Four surgeries, 126 days in the ICU, losing my ability to physically do anything, then gaining it all back was a blessing. I thought I would never be able to walk or talk again, but I was living proof that God was real.

I started with my lashes, taking those off next. I looked so funny without them, since I didn't have lashes of my own. My eyes begin to water, which was something I've done over the years. You would think I would be used to this by now, but I wasn't, and I still cried every night I reveal myself.

As I wiped the makeup from my neck, the tan colored spots slowly appeared. Slowly, I filled five makeup wipes with Fendi foundation, concealer, blush, and lipstick. I was erasing the image I betrayed to be daily. I was erasing who the world thought I was, and revealing who I truly am. One day, I would get the courage to live in my truth. One day, I would get the courage and the strength that I speak about; that I distill in others. As I looked in the mirror, I let the tears flow freely. It was a mixture of joy and pain. I missed me, I missed my beautiful skin. I missed how I looked before I almost lost my life. I missed the Zofiaa before my husband took his life, and attempted to take mine. It's been years, and I could still smell the scent of burning flesh. Thank God I was saved, or else I would have died with him that night.

Because of my dead ex-husband, I don't even talk to men. In fact, I'm absolutely terrified to even look at a man. I was living in my world where all men were the same to me. I knew it wasn't true, but I couldn't stop my mind from thinking that. I couldn't allow another man to get close to me, in fear that he would hurt me or worse kill me. Every little noise I heard in my house scared me. I had so many locks on my doors, that I prayed I never experienced a house fire. It would be damn near impossible for the firefighters to get in. I knew he was dead, but that didn't stop me from looking over my shoulders. Sometimes, it felt like I could still feel him near, and those days were the worse. I don't know where I got my strength from, but I was glad that I found it, and my voice. Speaking to women who have experienced, or is stuck in a relationship that's toxic, was a blessing. I wanted to share my story with as many as possible and save lives.

Zamaria was so beautiful and so full of life. She could literally, bounce back from all of this and be anything she wanted. I was so heartbroken listening to her story, and realizing she was heading down the road I fought so hard to protect her from. I wanted more for my baby. I wanted more for my daughter. I didn't want her to grow up living the life I did, and oddly, she was heading down that road. She didn't deserve that shit, and it tore me up to hear that a man has put his hands on her. I regretted making the decision I made; for years, I wished that I could have done things differently. If it was another way, anything else I could have done, then I would have. I never told anyone about it, about my daughter, because I really thought maybe she didn't make it. I thought she may have died, and it was my fault. I cried, and I cried, for what seemed like years. It got to a point where I eventually wanted to take my life. I second guessed leaving her the way I did, and I prayed so much that I was sure God was tired of me. But all of the praying, all of the crying, all of the years I fought for my life, God was gifting me with the only thing I've ever wanted, and that was to be a mother.

Zamaria spoke so intelligent, but with so much anger, so much pain. She had the right to express herself any way she sees fit. She had every right to be angry, and I couldn't blame her. She had so many questions that I knew the answers too, but I couldn't answer them. It wasn't that it was too soon, I was scared. I didn't know how she would take this information, or take me, for that matter. Walking to my bathroom, I turned on the shower. The only thing I wanted to do was relax and figure out a way to tell her. My phone beeped with a message, and I smiled when I realized who it was. The message said exactly what I asked of her, and I was glad to know she could follow directions. Now that I knew she was safe, I could relax a little.

I took a warm shower, since anything hot on my skin triggered my PTSD. Once I finished my shower, I slipped on my PJ's and went to the kitchen to get a glass of wine. When I returned to my bedroom, I had another message, which caught me by surprise. Reading over it, I got an idea. Sometimes you give out the advice

J'DIORR

you should take. Today, I felt like I did just that. Opening my night-stand, I pulled out a notebook and pen. I found a blank page and stared at it briefly, before picking up the pen and writing a letter to my daughter.

Dear A'miracle, but I know you as Zamaria. You're my daughter..."

ELEVEN

Tabari

---

*T*oday was the day I was dreading the most. I never wanted to see my uncle like this. Goodbye wasn't supposed to be like this, and still to this day, I wondered what could have been done differently. Camron didn't deserve this shit, and this is something a nigga will never get over. The only time I will have peace is the moment Wade's ass is six feet under. Just the thought of burying my uncle, and this bitch ass nigga, Wade, was still breathing, was fucking with my mental. I would have rather laid him to rest knowing Wade's ass was murked already. When you do bitch ass shit, you become a bitch ass nigga.

Pulling up to the funeral home, I was surprised when I saw people outside. I specifically said I wanted this to be private and small, and it looked like the whole hood was here.

"Who are all these people?" My mother asked, looking over at me.

"I don't know, Mama. People Camron knows," I said, hoping she didn't feed into it. On the outside I looked fine, but inside, I was pissed. I wondered how the word got out. I mean, the only people knew I was having the funeral today was Tazz, Meechie, and Choppa. Choppa's not from around here, so I know he didn't say shit. Hopefully, the other two didn't run their damn mouths. Either way, I had to go through with this. I wanted it private, because my mother and sister were here. I wanted my mother to take all the time she needed to say goodbye to her brother. I didn't wanna put my family in harm's way, at all. We were at war, and the last thing I needed was my family getting hurt in the process. I didn't even allow A'miracle to come, because I didn't need shit popping off again, and her going back down the road, she fought so hard to come from. I was so proud of her. She was going to her therapy sessions faithfully, and really developed a relationship with her therapist. I've never seen the woman, but I've heard nothing but wonderful things from A'miracle about her. As long as my baby was smiling, I supported everything she wanted to do.

The inside of the church was empty. As we walked down the aisle and closer to the casket, it felt like my heart was beating out of my chest. The yellow and blue flowers were scattered all around, and I couldn't believe this was really happening. The closer I got, the harder things became. Camron was all that I knew as a father figure. He taught me so much, and I was broken that his life ended the way that it did. I held my mother up as she cried for her brother. My sister was young, so she didn't really know what a funeral meant. Once my mother was settled and finally seated, they opened the doors and allowed others to mourn him. I watched everyone as they came to the casket to pay their respects. Most of these people I didn't know, but through it all, my uncle was indeed loved. There was even a couple of women claiming to be his wife, and I couldn't do shit but smirk as everything unfolded. The voice I heard next wasn't expected, and when I turned around, I almost lost it.

"Man, this shit not right!" Wade spat, as he staggered down to my uncle's casket. Before I had a chance to stop him or fuck him up, Choppa had his people front in center.

"Let me go, man! It wasn't supposed to be like this! I swear!" Wade spat, as the tears fell from his eyes. As I stood to my feet, so did Choppa, looking directly at me. He nodded his head and stared at me. I knew what he meant, and as bad as I didn't want to, I sat back down next to my family.

Wade's high ass was escorted out of the funeral, and I couldn't wait to get to his ass. Overall, everything ran smoothly. Before I knew it, the hardest part was before me. The pastor prayed as my uncle's casket was slid on the small metal poles. As the casket was lowered to the ground, people began to cry, I knew this was the end. My uncle lived no more, but I will make sure his legacy does. They shouted my uncle's name as I continued to watch him get lowered to his final resting place. Tears slipped from my eyes and I quickly wiped them away. I said a quick prayer to myself, before helping my mother back to the limo. She didn't want to throw a repast. Instead, she said she would cook a big Sunday dinner, and I was pleased with that. I didn't feel like being around people, showing fake love. Majority of people show up at funerals to eat, be nosy, and basically, start some shit. Since Wade popped up and embarrassed not only himself, but my family, I'm sure everyone is waiting around to see what I'm going to do. That's a problem. Now I couldn't fuck the nigga up, because if I do, it could lead back to me.

"Aren't you staying for a while?" My mother asked, as soon as we walked inside her door.

"Nah, Ma, I gotta head out and handle some things," I expressed, trying my best not to make eye contact with her. I didn't wanna lie to my mother, and I never did.

"Listen, I don't want you to-"

"Ma, I'm fine. I will be ok, please. Just let me go handle what's needed. I'll be back tomorrow," I said, kissing her forehead and heading towards the door.

"Don't forget about dinner Sunday, and bring that girl. I wanna meet the woman who has my son's heart," my mother said, causing me to turn and smile at her.

"I'm serious. I know she means a lot to you; it's all over your face. A mother knows, so bring her with you. I'll cook up your favorites, and tell Keahi to come with a date. It's time my boys settled down. I'm getting old, and I need to make sure these women y'all dating learns how to make the food just like y'all like it. So, when I'm gone-"

"Ma! Please don't talk like that. You're not going anywhere.

Besides, God will send you back," I said, laughing, as I opened the front door.

"You're right about that. Be careful, son, I love you," my mother expressed.

"I love you too, Ma."

~

I pulled up at the location Choppa texted me with nothing but vengeance in my heart. I tried talking with God on the way over here, and asking Him to control the beast that lived within me, but it was a waste of time. I knew in my heart I was going to kill this man, and no one could stop me. As I walked up to the door and opened it, I couldn't help the sensation that came over me. It was like I was hungry for blood, and the only way to fulfill my appetite was to give it exactly what it craved. I already changed my clothes after I left my mother's house. I had on M.A.N (murk a nigga) gear, and was ready to put in work.

As I walked down the stairs and through the plastic, I could feel cold air and could hear Choppa's voice. When Wade saw me, his face went pale, like Casper, and the nigga pissed his pants. I don't know what came over me, but the moment I saw him, the bottom of my boot connected with his face, sending him flying backward. Luckily, the chair he was tied to broke his fall, and my boot damn near dislocated his jaw.

"Bitch ass nigga! That's for putting your hands on a woman; my woman, to be exact," I said, as I leaned over him. Spade laughed as he stood in the corner eating a bag of sunflower seeds.

"Man, my business with my bitch, is my business. She got her ass whooped for being in your face, nigga," Wade said, trying to show he actually had balls. Picking my foot up, I kicked his ass again.

"Agh! Fuck!" Wade spat, as the blood leaked from his nose.

"It's taking everything in me not to blow your fucking brains out," I spat, spitting in his face.

"Why'd you do it?" I asked, looking him dead in his eyes. I could sense that he was searching for the right words to say, and for his sake, I prayed he found them.

"I don't know what you talking about," Wade responded, trying to play stupid. I grabbed the sides of the chair and lifted it, putting him back in the upright position. I had to calm myself down before I shot this nigga in his face. It was taking everything in me not to do it, but I needed answers first.

"It wasn't supposed to be like this," Wade said, as he spit blood on the floor. I could see his eyes getting watery, and wondered why niggas cried when it was time to pay up. I mean, he was just this big shot ass nigga, now he was a straight bitch! When you do dirt, dirt comes back to you. The least he could have done was go out like a G. I crossed my arms and shook my head, observing how pitiful Wade was. To keep me from slapping the shit out of him., I had to take a few steps backward. We were in a freezer at an old bakery. If Wade thought this shit would be easy, that his death would be over quick, or that I would show any mercy, his ass had another thing coming.

"I didn't mean for this to happen, Tabari. I swear, I didn't. Them nigga killed him on purpose and-"

"Yea, cause you paid them to do it! Fuck type of snake shit you on? That man did everything for you! Everything, and this the thanks he gets!" I yelled, getting upset. I unzipped my jacket and took it off, since I felt hot. I only had a wife beater on underneath.

"Listen, Tabari, I didn't want this. All I wanted was to show him I was capable of handling business; that's it. I swear! I never meant for him to die. Honestly, I just wanted to shake him up a little, not kill him! That's not what I paid them for. He was supposed to be a little fucked up, that way, he couldn't work. I would be the one handling everything, and by the time he came back, he would see how I was successfully handling business, and get out for good. I didn't need a motherfucker looking over my shoulder," Wade's stupid ass said, and without thinking, I kicked his ass again. This time, I knocked the wind out of him. I waited for his pain to subside before I spoke.

"You set my uncle up, even after he planned to give you everything. That's greed, my nigga. My uncle paved the way for Biggs's to make money! He would have given you anything, and you know this! You took his life, because shit wasn't going the way you planned, or at the rate you wanted it to go. Bitch ass niggas like you are the reason the streets fucked up now! Where's the loyalty, my nigga? All you had to do was wait your turn! You could have made a ton of bread with Cameron, my nigga, but you decided to cross him! You took his life, for what? Look at the position you in now! No one respects you, and they never will! Not only do you have me on your ass, but the niggas you paid wants your ass dead! On top of all that, you lost your bitch to me, dog. Weighing everything, it looks like you losing drastically, my nigga. Oh, and Lazer killed your sister, if you didn't know," I spat, as I walked over to him.

"Wait, what? Dove's dead?" Wade asked, as he stared off into space.

"She's dead, toe tag, cold as a penguins ass. Damn, you really a fucked-up, nigga. I'm guessing you didn't know her throat got slit. It was probably because of your dumb ass anyway," Spade said, spitting seed shells everywhere.

"Bear, it wasn't like that. I never meant for any of this shit to happen. Yea, I was jealous, but I knew what Mack promised me. Then when that changed, and something that was supposed to be mine, became mine and someone else's, I snapped. I felt like C-Mack was playing me. Like I need some type of babysitter or some shit. Tazz ass ain't do none of the shit I did, but here he was, getting ready to take over an empire with me! How? I earned this shit! All this shit was supposed to be mine! How the fuck do you think I should feel?" Wade yelled, getting some balls. I kicked his ass in his face this time, and I heard his nose pop. The yell that echoed off the walls around me was something I needed to here. It was the fuel I needed.

"Aghhh! Man, stop please," Wade cried.

"Stop? Did this nigga really say that? At least die with some dignity, my nigga. These niggas straight bitches these days. How you commit a murder, well, pay someone to do it for you, then beg for your life? What sense does that make?" Spade's high ass stated, laughing. He was getting a kick out of this shit, but I wasn't joking. The moment I pulled my gun out and cocked it back, my phone vibrated. It was Tazz.

"Yo?" I said, listening to him.

"Wait, you sure?" I asked, looking over at Choppa.

"Aight, we on the way," I spoke, hanging up.

"What's up, fam?" Choppa asked.

"Tazz got eyes on Lazer. He's alone," I said, walking back over and putting on my jacket. I then called Meechie and told him to meet me here. It took him ten minutes to make it to where we were. When he walked inside and saw Wade, his eyes got big.

"I thought this nigga was dead," Meechie said, looking at me.

"Yea, he will be soon. Keep an eye on him 'til we get back," I said, handing a gun to Meechie, and going out of the door. We all hopped in Choppa's truck and headed in the direction Tazz gave us. This nigga was in the hood, at one of the best hood joints, and also, one of the worse. El Grande is a Mexican place on the west side of Chicago. It has the best cheesesteak fries in town. Plenty of mother-fuckers walked in to place their orders, and never got to eat it. Never made it out of the parking lot, actually. I'm surprised they still up and running with so many people being shot in killed in the same spot. From where we were parked, I had the perfect view. I could see Lazer standing off to the side, waiting for his order. There was a lady in there with a toddler and an older cat. Bullets don't have names on them, and I would hate to take an innocent life.

"That's his car, right?" Spade asked, pointing.

"Yea, that's it. Tazz parked next to it," I said, pointing to Tazz's car. He had tented windows, so you couldn't see in that bitch.

"So, what you wanna do? Murk this MF now, or wait until he comes out?" Choppa asked, looking over at me. I wanted to murk his ass now, but feared harming someone else in the process. I knew personally how it felt to lose a loved one to gun violence, and didn't wanna bring the same pain to another family.

"Wait, follow his ass when he pulls off," I spat, resting my Glocks on my lap. I hope I made the right call, and this nigga won't get away.

"Aight, look," Spade said, pointing to Lazer. He grabbed the bag from the window, checked his food, and headed towards the door. I quickly called Tazz and told him what was up. I watched as Lazer walked over to his car and stood there. He looked around as if he felt someone watching him. He paused for a second, then opened his car door and got in. Moments later, he bagged out of the parking lot and went down the alley. Tazz was right one his tail, and once he made it to Central, he took off.

"Fuck!" I spat, realizing this nigga was running. Making it two streets over, he made a sharp right on a two-way side street. He damn near hit the car waiting to turn, as we followed closely behind him.

"He's trying to get to his part of town! We gotta blow this bitch!" I yelled, hoping Choppa sped up the pace. Lazer's car turned left, and so did Tazz, clipping the back of Lazer's car, sending him spinning into a light pole. Lazer's car hit the pole, and knocked the street lights out. Instantly, Choppa threw his car in park, and we all hopped out. Lazer's car was smoking, as I approached it with caution. All niggas had straps on them and in their cars. Pulling on the door handle, I yanked it a few times before it opened. Lazer was slumped over the steering wheel. I slapped his ass a few times, and pushed his head back into the seat. I saw his gun on the floor on the passenger side.

"Wake yo' bitch ass up, nigga," I provoked, tugging his chest with my Glock. I watched as his eyes fluttered, before he finally opened them. He had a gash on the top of his head and was leaking pretty bad. When he saw my face, this nigga didn't do shit but smirk.

"Yea, nigga, Grim Reaper in the flesh. This for my uncle," I yelled, sending a slug in his chest. He moaned in pain, but the smirk never left his face.

"This for my bitch," I said, shooting him twice in his face. Brain batter scattered all over the dashboard as we ran back to the cars. I got inside and noticed Tazz was in his trunk. He pulled out a gas can and poured it all over Lazer, before pulling out a lighter. Tazz took a step back, flicked the lighter, and threw it on Lazer, causing him and the car to go up in flames.

"Bail out!" Choppa yelled, as Tazz hopped in his car and sped off. We flew from one end of the city to the next, taking all side streets. My adrenaline was rushing, and the only thing I wanted to do now was kill Wade's ass, and take my woman on a trip. I got my uncle's revenge, and now I needed to get my girls. We parked on the side of the building Wade was being held in and we all walked inside.

"Good shit, fam," Choppa said to me, but I don't feel good. I mean, I did, but it's not like it would bring Camron back. Then, on the other hand, there was no way in hell I could let that shit slide. I wasn't the type of nigga that would take an L like that.

"Yea, thanks," I said, as we walked through the plastic and into the freezer.

"Fuck!" I yelled, the moment I saw Meechie laying on his back. Blood was everywhere, and Wade was nowhere in sight.

"Meechie! Come on, kid!" Tazz yelled, slapping his face. His chest was covered in blood, and I knew he was dead.

"Fuck!" I spat, turning and looking at Choppa. Now we gotta go on a manhunt to find this nigga and get his ass, before he got one of us…

TWELVE

Wade

————————

J was so exhausted from running through alley's, but I had to keep going if I wanted to live. I knew Tabari would come back and kill me; there was no doubt in my mind about it. I was lucky that Tabari received a phone call and left. The moment I saw who would be watching me, I knew my life was on the count down, and I needed to think of something fast. Meechie was a street kid by heart. I knew personally that he has always wanted to prove himself; like most street kids did. They wanna show that they're about that life, catch a couple of bodies, make their bosses proud, and possibly move up the chain. Meechie was one of those kids, and I had to test his savage.

I started fucking with him, telling him that he will always be in the same place he's in now. No one would take him seriously, which is why he's always a babysitter. That pissed him off. I could sense it in his body movement. He ignored me for a while, well, as long as he could, but I knew exactly what to do to get the reaction I needed. I fucked with his mind; simply trying to get him to untie me. I knew if he did that, then I would have the upper hand, and could possibly make it out of here alive. I talked about his family, called his mother all types of bitches. He hit me a few times when I called him a hoe. I told him that he wouldn't dare do that shit to me if I wasn't tied to this chair. I had his ass so mad and hot, that he untied me. The moment I felt my arms get loose, I launched at his ass. We tussled for a while, before I got the best of him. I damn near knocked him out, and took that time to grab the gun that slid across the floor. I stood over his ass and shot him. I don't know how many times I shot him, but I knew he was dead. I took all the money out of his pockets and his bus card. I figured I'd have to find my way to my destination using public transportation, and run the rest of the way.

Tabari's ass had a lot of nerve talking about this is for his bitch. A'miracle's ass knew where her home was, and once I got on my feet and built a solid team, I was going back to get my bitch. She needed another ass whooping to remind her of her place. If she thought the first few times were bad, wait until I got my hands on her this time. Running around the city with another nigga when you got a whole nigga. How? I knew at first, I was having regrets about beating her ass, now I don't, and I knew once I got my hands on her this time I would do it again. I made it to Pulaski just as the bus pulled up. I knew people were looking at me like I was crazy, since I was fucked up. I made little to no eye contact and scanned the card.

"Scan your card again, sir," the bus driver said. Instead of trying to figure out if it was money on the card or not, I simply grabbed a five-dollar bill to pay my fair, and walked to the back of the bus. I sat low in the window seat, hoping nobody driving pass would spot me. I had a gash on the side of my head, and my jaw was in so much pain, I was sure it was broken. I didn't know what to do, or where to go, until something hit me. I knew exactly where I could go, and hopefully, get help.

It's crazy how a motherfucker would do you dirty, then try to come back into your life. I ignored her the first time I saw her, and when she approached me, I think I was in shock. So many nights I thought about killing my mother if I ever saw her again. She doesn't realize the shit she put my sister and me through, all over a nigga. I was forced to provide and make sure I kept Dove out of harm's way, now I couldn't help the thought of having her blood on my hands. I knew Lazer was someone I didn't wanna fuck with! I knew this shit, but in my mind, I had things handled.

I was going to pay him and Choppa, but shit didn't work out the way I had it planned. I fucked up big time, and it literally, cost my sister's life. Although we weren't on good terms, hell, you can even say we hated each other, I never wanted her to be killed. Especially when it came to me, and was partially my fault, I didn't want to live with that on my conscience. I made it to the blue line train station. I got on the train within ten minutes and headed to Forest Park. I remembered her address, and knew that no one would come looking for me in the rich folk's neighborhoods. Forest Park held a variety of folks, but it looked nothing like the hood. I walked up Washington Street for what seemed like forever, before I finally made it to her door. My head was pounding, and I prayed she was home. Not wanting to stand in an area I wasn't familiar with, or for someone to look out of their window and call the police on me, I rang her bell. I wasn't sure what time it was, since I didn't have a phone. I stood in the doorway praying she would answer, and she did.

"Hello, who is it?" My mother's shaky voice said. I knew it was late, and I probably woke her up.

"Hey, umm, it's me, Wade, Mom. Can I come up? I need you," I said, and within seconds, the door buzzed. I quickly walked inside and up the stairs. She was on the third floor. The moment she saw me, she covered her mouth. I couldn't even make it to her door before I collapsed. I passed out for a brief moment, and when I woke up, she was over me.

"Come on, get inside," my mother instructed, helping me to my feet. She led me over to the couch before running back to the door and locking it. I watched as she made sure all her blinds were closed, before she turned on the lights. She was moving so damn fast, that it was starting to scare me. I didn't ask who was here with her, and since I was on the edge, I couldn't take any chances. I pulled the gun from my waist and placed it on my lap. She returned with towels, and a boat load of other shit that she managed to drop when she saw the gun.

"Wh-what's that's for?" My mother asked, looking at me.

"Protection. Anyone here with you?" I asked, not trying to frighten my mother, but let her know I was ready, and will kill a motherfucker. With the shit I've been through, I couldn't trust a soul right now. It was like I was walking around with a bounty on my head.

"No, Wade, I'm alone. I live by myself. No one is here," her crackling voice responded. I nodded my head and closed my eyes, trying to endure the pain. It felt like my entire body was on fire.

"Let me help you, clean you up a bit," my mother said, but was kind of asking. I nodded my head again, and watched as she picked up everything she dropped. Neither of us said anything while she cleaned and bandaged the gash on my head.

"Here, take these pills," she said, handing me two small blue pills she was holding in her hands. I wasn't trying to be mean, but right now, I couldn't trust anyone. I didn't know if these were real pain pills, or something to knock me out.

"I'd rather not. You have any alcohol?" I asked, causing her to look at me funny. She came back into the living room holding a half a bottle of tequila. I took it, popped the top off, and gulped it down.

"Slow down! That's not going to help you at all," my mother suggested, causing me to snap.

"Shut the fuck up. You don't know what will help!" I yelled, catching her off guard. Realizing I overreacted, I apologized to her.

"I'm sorry. I'm just in a really fucked up situation," I said. Not wanting to vent and tell her too much, I changed the subject.

"Why'd you leave us?" I asked, looking at her. Instead of standing, she chose to sit next to me. This is something that has been on my mind the moment she walked out of that door. I saved my sister that day, and in return, our mother walked out on us.

"I wasn't strong, son; I just wasn't. Back then, the only thing I valued was drugs, and any and everybody to make sure I got it," she said, which really wasn't an answer in my book.

"Yea, but you valued that shit over your kids, Ma? What sense does that make?"

"Wade, it doesn't make sense at all, and I really can't explain the

J'DIORR
reason I made the decisions I did. I was only looking out for my best interest, and that was being with a man that could guarantee I'd get my fix whenever I needed it," she said, with tears in her eyes.

"Dominique, he raped your daughter. He raped my sister, and you did nothing about it. You knew Dove told me she told you," I said, feeling myself getting upset. I guess she did too, since she quickly stood to her feet.

"I don't wanna talk about Dove. She's no longer here to defend herself," my mother said, causing me to look at her like she was crazy. Before I knew it, I snapped.

"Fuck you mean?! She told you about this shit, and instead of getting rid of your rapist ass boyfriend, you chose to turn your back on your kids! The fucking streets sucked my ass in, Ma, they own me! This wasn't the life I thought I have. Definitely not the fucking life I wanted to live or prayed for. Do you realize the shit I had to go through? The shit I had to do as a child? Just to make sure my sister had food on the table. You left us with nothing. How could you call yourself a mother?" I spoke with so much pain.

"Now wait a minute! You will not come to my house for help, and disrespect me! I know what the fuck I've done, and what I didn't do! I know the mistakes I made, and I also know I've prayed and changed my life around. You're not God, so who the fuck are you to judge me, Wade? You were supposed to protect her! You! She trusted you as her brother, and you let her down! This is not just on me for leaving, you fucking let her down too!" My mother cried, causing me to pick up my gun and point it at her.

"Oh, so that's what the kids are doing out on the streets, shooting their mothers? Well, go ahead! That's what you wanted to do anyway. Go ahead, pull the fucking trigger! Any place but here will be so much better than the hell I'm living in," my mother said, as the tears rolled down her cheek. Her tears meant nothing to me, just like her word. Without warning, I gave her ass exactly what she asked for, and pulled the trigger…

90

THIRTEEN

A' miracle

———————————

*M*y father was doing a little better, but still wasn't out of harm's way. He really needed a kidney, and I prayed he received a donor soon. As for my life, it seemed like everything has taken a turn for the better. My company was doing good, although I was still working from home, and occasionally Starbucks. Mr. Martinez apologized, gave me ten thousand dollars, and I haven't seen him since. Tabari and I developed a don't ask, don't tell rule, about certain shit, and that was one of the situations. From the looks of Mr. Martinez's face, he got a well-deserved ass whooping. Either way, I wasn't complaining. My therapy sessions were amazing, and each time I left feeling refreshed. It kinda felt like I've known Zofiaa forever. We just clicked, and the bond we were building was amazing.

My mother was jealous, cause she said we spent an awful lot of time together, and I thought it was funny. She was the one who agreed to me speaking to a professional when I told her, and now, she didn't want me to. I think that my father's condition was taking a toll on her, and in a weird way, she felt as if she was slowly losing me too. It's true, Zofiaa and I did spend a lot of time together, and I didn't mind it. She felt like I was the daughter she didn't get have.

She told me about her domestic violence relationship, and the day she had to make a difficult decision and almost lost her life. Whatever decision that was, she never shared, and I didn't press the issue. I felt like some things are still tough for women like us to talk about, and when the time was right, she would tell me.

Now I was standing in front of the mirror second guessing my outfit. Tabari invited me over to his mother's house for Sunday dinner, and I wanted to make the perfect first impression. Our relationship was getting deeper, and I won't say I don't love him, but I wasn't going to say it first. I mean, all of the signs were there. He was so compassionate, sincere, he put my wants before his, and was protective of me. I couldn't even sigh without him dropping everything and coming to my aid. He really had me spoiled, and was always doing things to make me feel appreciated. He cared about my feelings, encouraged me when I felt like giving up. He even told me that my days of working in the house will be all over soon. I didn't know what that meant, but if this man brought me a building for my company, I'd probably lose it. I decided to wear a sleeveless navy deep v dress. It hugged my curves just enough to keep Tabari's eyes on me, but was respectful enough to meet his mother. I paired them with a nude pump and matching purse. Fashion Nova knew they had some hot shit, but just took all day to deliver. I got my hair done in a straight part down the middle and nice light curls. It's been a minute since I dressed it all up, and was actually happy.

"You nervous?" Tabari asked, walking behind me, and kissing the side of my neck. This man's lips were so soft, that I was tempted to take all this shit off and fuck him 'til the wee hours of the morning. Hell, Sunday dinner leftovers are always good. Quickly shaking the nasty thoughts from my head, I just smiled at him. God, how did I get so lucky? To end a completely bad and toxic relationship, and manage to get everything I've ever wanted in a new man. Just to think about it, I was giving Tabari such a hard time when we first met; when he was simply trying to be my friend. Not knowing he would be my knight in shining armor, and actually save my life. God knows I was so ready to give up on life. I wanted so badly to give up on love, but now looking at the great man that stood behind me, I'm so glad I didn't. Damn, I was lucky.

"You have nothing to be nervous about. My mom is sweet, and my sister, you're going to fall in love with her. She's such a strong little girl, despite her condition. She doesn't let the odds beat her. She beats the odds. She's very independent, and does a lot on her own. You'd be surprised. You look good, by the way, too damn good," Tabari spat, slapping my ass.

"Ouch! That hurt, bae," I whined, turning and kissing his lips.

"Don't worry, I'll kiss it later and make it feel all better," he said, sticking his tongue out and flicking it. Just the thought of his tongue on me in any way, made me want to slide my panties to the side.

"I can't wait, but we're going to be late," I said, looking at the time. It was well after five, and dinner started at six.

"It's fine, Mom knows I'm always a little behind, plus, I'm not sure if everyone is there yet," Tabari said, confusing me.

"Don't worry, A'miracle, everyone is going to love you. It's just Keahi and Eternity, and one of my mom's old friends, Fee-Fee, from school. I'm not sure if she has a date coming, and my sister. Now, if Mom just so happened to invite other folks, then I don't know. She didn't tell me, but your man will be right next to you. I won't leave your side. Plus, I'll play with your pussy under the dinner table to keep you calm, and make you cum," Tabari smirked, with his nasty ass. I loved every bit of it though. He was rocking a navy button-up shirt, cream slacks, and navy loafers. We looked damn good together. I was a complement of his strength, his love, and I looked damn good on his arm. We took a few pictures that I posted on Facebook before heading out of the door. I was excited about meeting his family, and even more excited to see where our relationship was heading. Call me crazy for jumping out on faith and attempting the love again, but I did, and I've never felt more complete in my life.

When we arrived at Tabari's house, I had to pee. I didn't even get a chance to greet his mother yet, since she was in the kitchen. So far, from what I've seen, the house was absolutely beautiful. It held a cozy feeling, and reminded me of my grandparent's home. The aroma of the soul food filled the air, and I couldn't wait to eat. Lord knows I've been wanting some greens and baked mac and cheese and sweet potatoes for the longest, but I didn't wanna cook it. I was definitely about to throw down at the dinner table.

Tabari showed me where the bathroom was, and I took my time to calm my nerves. I was usually good at talking to people and just being myself, so I don't know why I was so nervous. Then again, I did. I never met Wade's parents, so I didn't have to go through this. This would be my first encounter with someone's parents, and I wanted to make sure I impressed them. I wouldn't spend a lot of time talking about myself and my accomplishments, because that's showing off and can come off a bit rude. I knew Tabari loved and cared for his mother and sister so much, that it made me wish I had an older brother. The way he drops everything when they call, there was no denying the bond they shared. I just wanted his mother to know that her son was safe with me, and I would love him for the rest of his life if he allowed me to. When I walked out of the bathroom, I was greeted by his little sister. Tabari was right, she was such a cutie pie.

"Hello," I smiled down at the little girl. Her ponytails were so long and thick. I wondered what type of products his mother used in her hair. By being natural, I would love to get my hair thicker.

"Hello, you're my brother's girlfriend," she said, with the biggest smile on her face. I had to laugh, since she seemed so excited to say that to me.

"Yes, I am. And you're my boyfriend's little sister, Tiana, right?" I said, watching her face light up.

"You know my name, and I know yours too. It's A'miracle," she beamed, smiling even more.

"Yes, you are right, sweetie. Did you need help with anything?" I asked, as I moved out of the way and helped her go inside the bathroom.

"Nope, I can do it. Just save me a seat next to you," she smiled, before closing the door. I couldn't help but smile since she was so perfect. Tabari was right, Tiana's condition didn't define her at all. She was such a strong little girl, and I adored her already. I walked back down the hall and admired the pictures of Tabari's family. It reminded me of my mother and all the pictures she has around the house of us. Making it back to the living room, I stood there, since I was afraid to walk inside the kitchen. I guess my man could feel my presence, since he stuck his head out and motioned for me to come over to him.

"Mom, Fe-Fe, I would love for you to meet my girlfriend, A'miracle," Tabari expressed, kissing my lips. It felt like my words got caught in my throat the moment I saw Zofiaa.

"Well, don't just stand there, girl. Give your mother in law some love. Oh, she is beautiful, Tabari. I love her already," Tabari's mother said, hugging me.

"Thank you so much for having me. Your home is lovely, and it smells so good," I smiled, breaking our embrace and turning to face Zofiaa.

"How are you doing today, A'miracle? My God, this is a small world," Zofiaa laughed, before hugging me.

"Did you finish your letter?" She asked.

"Yes, I did. I got everything out I wanted to say within five pages," I smiled, as she squeezed my hand.

"Wait, you guys know each other?" Tabari asked, with a confused expression plastered on his face.

"I'm sorry, baby, this is my therapist. Crazy, right? Definitely a small world," I responded.

"Well, how about you ladies get comfortable in the living room, and I'll bring you both some wine?" Tabari said, kissing my forehead just as the bell rung. Zofiaa and I walked to the living room and took a seat. Tabari opened the door, and Eternity and Keahi walked in. I was so excited to see my best friend. Since we both were in a happy relationship now, most of our time was spent tending to our men then each other. I would definitely plan us a real girl's trip, or maybe a couple's trip, since I knew neither Tabari or Keahi would let us out of their sights. Once everyone was introduced, we all sat in the living room, cracking jokes and drinking wine. The room was filled with nothing but love, and I was excited to be a part of it.

"Dinner is served," Tabari's mother said, as we all got up and went to the table. My God, this woman could throw down. I haven't seen this much food since Thanksgiving. I literally, didn't know where to start. She had baked chicken, BBQ beef short ribs, yams, ham, greens, baked mac and cheese, cornbread, spaghetti, apple pie, and strawberry cheesecake.

"Tabari, would you say grace, son?" His mother asked, as we all held hands. I saved a spot for Tiana, just as she requested it. I closed my eyes as my man's voice echoed off the walls around me.

"God, thank you so much for giving me exactly what I needed, family and real love. Today we sit and feast together as one. God, I ask that you bless the food before us, bless the family beside us, and bless the love between us. In Jesus name, we pray, Amen," Tabari said, as we all opened our eyes.

"That was short and sweet, now it's time to eat!" Keahi's goofy ass stated, causing us all to burst into laughter. As I sat down, my phone vibrated, alerting me of an email, but I didn't want to be rude, so I ignored it. We all made our plates and were enjoying great conversation and amazing food. But the moment the hospital called, I couldn't ignore it, and excused myself from the table. It was Dr. Kirby, explaining that they found a match, and I should have the email. I thanked him and made my way back to the table.

"Is everything ok, babe?" Tabari asked, causing everyone to look at me. I knew he could tell something was wrong, but I didn't want to ruin dinner. I'd tell him everything once we got home.

"Umm, yea, yea. It's fine," I said, displaying a weak smile that he didn't buy. I really didn't know how to feel, honestly. I mean, everything I've wanted is in this email, but was I ready to open it? The moment I felt his hand on my leg and squeezing it for comfort, I felt more relaxed than anxious.

"Aht! Aht! We are family, and I can see that something isn't right. You wanna talk about it?" Tabari's mother asked. Not wanting to bring my personal issues to the table, I looked over at Zofiaa, who nodded in agreeance with Tabari's mother. This was something Zofiaa and I had been practicing, being able to communicate quicker. If something is wrong, I should state that, instead of holding it in. It would only make things worse. But was now the right time for this?

"Well, I'm adopted, and I wanted to reach out to my biological parents," I said, causing Zofiaa to choke.

"You ok, Fe? Here, drink some water," Tabari's mother said, passing a bottle to her. I waited for her to calm herself and wondered if this conversation was something, I should have spoken to Tabari about privately. Maybe even Zofiaa?

"You know, now isn't the time. I'll handle it later," I said, drinking a sip of wine.

"No, sweetie, it's ok. You can share with us," Tabari's mother insisted. I didn't wanna be rude, so I continued my story.

"My adoptive parents found me in a box outside of the fire station my adoptive father worked. Long story short, they didn't have children. The baby they did have, died. She was stillborn," I explained, watching the faces of the people around me.

"My adoptive mother went through depression, and I basically saved her life, just as well as she saved mine. I learned I was adopted at the hospital, in a weird, yet funny, kind of way," I said, laughing, looking around at everyone.

"At first, I was upset, but looking at the bigger picture and the number of kids that are being killed and or left for dead, I was blessed that a family chose me. I just felt that something was missing, you know? I had a lot of unanswered questions that my adoptive parents couldn't answer, but my biological parents could. So, I wanted to reach out to my parents. Because of this and a lot of other things that happened in my life recently, I decided to go to therapy. That's where I met Zofiaa," I said, smiling at her, and wiping the tears out the corner of my eye.

"I know this is a lot, and I'm probably rambling, we could just-"

"No, sweetie, it's perfectly fine to share your story. To live in your truth. Isn't that what you always say, Zofiaa?" Tabari's mother asked. Zofiaa just nodded her head. I could tell she was a little uneasy, but I didn't know why. Tabari's mother insisted I continued, and I didn't wanna be rude to her, so I did.

"Basically, I went down to a DNA place that Dr. Kirby

suggested. I was on the phone with him when I stepped away. They found a match, and I have the email. I'm not sure if I want to open it yet," I said, looking over at Tabari. He quickly kissed my forehead, then my lips, before wrapping his arms around me.

"Baby girl, you listen to me, God makes no mistakes. It's a reason for us all to be in this room right now, right here together. You could have gotten that email at any given day, at any given time, so why now? Maybe He needed you to be in the room filled with love, family, and possibly answers you're looking for. Open it," Tabari's mother said, looking at me, then over at Zofiaa. She spoke so clearly, and with so much compassion in her voice, that it made me feel safe. Picking up my phone, I opened the email. As I read over the email, it felt like my heart would beat out of my chest. There it was, my father's name, and I couldn't believe it.

"What's it say?" Tiana asked, causing us to laugh a little. The anticipation in the room was thick as I wiped a tear from the side of my eye before I responded.

"It says my father's name is Dakota Sss. I can't pronounce his last name. Can you tell me what this says, bae?" I asked, handing my phone to Tabari, but before he could respond, Zofiaa did.

"Saxe. Your father's last name was Saxe," Zofiaa said, as the tears ran freely. I was confused as to how she knew this information.

"My God," Tabari said, as he looked at my phone, and over at Zofiaa. I was confused, since it looked as if his face went blank.

"What? What is it?" I asked, wondering what the hell was going on.

"Your mother's name is here as well," Tabari said, handing the phone back to me. When I read the name, it felt like my words got caught in my throat. I looked over at Zofiaa, and knew exactly why she was crying. I didn't know how to feel at this very moment, so I cried with her.

"Zofiaa, what's your last name?" Tabari's mother asked, holding her hand.

"Saxe. I'm Zofiaa Saxe. I'm your biological mother, A'miracle," she said, as the entire table gasped.

"Hey, Tiana, maybe you should show me the new game Tabari

got you. Think I can beat you?" Keahi asked, standing and walking over to Tiana.

"Nah, I'm too good," she smiled, as they both left the table, leaving me, Tabari, Zofiaa, Eternity, and his mother.

"I knew who you were. I felt it in my heart," Zofiaa said, as if that made anything better.

"Why didn't you say anything? You knew all along and didn't say nothing," I spat, feeling myself getting upset.

"I didn't know how. I knew you were upset, and I felt that you needed me to be your therapist first, before your mother," Zofiaa said, sounding crazy.

"How could you? You looked me in my face, and watched me express my feeling about not knowing who my biological parents were. You watched me cry about them, praying that God provided me with some type of answers, and you knew all alone. How cruel can you be?" I spat, shaking my head.

"Can I explain, please? I mean, you wanted answers, and I'm the only one who could give them to you," Zofiaa stated, which was true.

"Was it true? Any of it? What you told me that happened to you, was it true?" I cried, as Tabari did his best to comfort me.

"Yes, I was in a domestic violence relationship with your father, and he tried to kill me. That is very much true," Zofiaa stated, in a voice where I had no choice but to believe her. I covered my face and sobbed, because I couldn't believe this. None of it was making sense, and I was trying my best not to lose it. I heard the chair move next to me, and when I looked to my left, Zofiaa was sitting right next to me. She grabbed my hands from my face and held them in hers. As mad as I was, I allowed her to.

"A'miracle, your real name is Zamaria Saxe. I named you that because I thought it was really pretty, and it matched you. Your father, Dakota, beat me every day, all the way up until I gave birth to you. He has done some unimaginable things, leaving scars neither of us could get rid of," Zofiaa stated, slowly taking off the netted sweater she had on. She placed her arm on the table, and I couldn't believe my eyes. Her scar matched mine. We had the same scar on the same arm.

"He burned us with a wire hanger. He said that we needed to know our place, and know that we belonged to him. The day that your father died, he talked about killing us both that entire weekend, and I couldn't let him harm you anymore. He complained that you cried too much, and if I didn't find a way to shut you up, he would do it for me. I was scared, Zamaria. I was scared that one day he would beat me until I passed out, and I would wake up and you would be dead. So, I had to make a decision," she said, looking down at the floor.

"I didn't want to give you away. I swear, I didn't. You were the only thing keeping me grounded, keeping me living. I snuck out of the house one night while he was passed out high. I knew I couldn't go far. I saw the fire station, and I knew someone was always there. I prayed so hard that day, my God, I did," Zofiaa said, as the tears continued to roll from her face.

"I kissed you for what felt like the last time, before I placed you in the box. I couldn't wait around to see if someone would come, because I didn't want to go back to jail. I went to jail for your father on drug charges. It was my first time, so I was out within a week. Your father has a history of charges, which is why his information popped up, beside the fact that he's dead. He tried to kill me, and you gave me the strength I needed to live, so I-"

"You killed him," I stated, finishing the sentence for her. Instantly, Zofiaa got up and walked down the hall. I could hear her rambling through something, and moments later, she returned holding make up wipes.

"Free me," she whispered, handing the wipes to me. I shook my head no, and she opened them for me and placed one in my hand.

"Please, my child, free me. Allow me to finish this story in my truths. Allow me to live in my truths," she stated. With a shaky hand, I slowly wiped her chin, removing the makeup. As I cleaned the makeup from her face, uncovering who she really was, she continued her story.

"The doctors thought I wasn't going to make it. I was burned so badly. I had numerous surgeries, and they honestly couldn't understand why my heart was still beating. I remember your father throwing me down the stairs and dragging me to the kitchen. I remember him tossing gasoline all over the place, including me. It stung so bad, even before it was lit. He did this to me! He took away my identity, and left me like this. I shot him, and just as I did, he lit a match and fell on top of me. I tried my hardest to get him off me as the smell of burning flesh filled the room. If it wasn't for one of my neighbors at the time, I would have died with him. I remember screaming so loud, then nothing else came out. I was in so much pain that I couldn't even express it. Because of him, because of Dakota, because of your father, is why I look like this," she said, as I finished up. Her skin was discolored all over. It was pink in some spots and brown in the others. I watched as she pulled her lashes, off then took off her wig. My God, I couldn't do anything but cry harder, finally knowing who my mother really was and the things she's been through. Zofiaa wrapped her arms around me, and we both sobbed together. Moments later, I felt another pair of hands, then another, and weight. As I looked up, I was in an embrace from not only Zofiaa, but everyone that was in the room. There wasn't a dry eye here. After we got ourselves together, and Zofiaa wiped a few of my tears away, I didn't know what to say. I was overwhelmed with so many emotions.

"What does this mean? Where do we go from here?" I asked, looking around.

"It means, you no longer have to wonder who your biological mother is, because she's sitting right in front of you. It means that God works in mysterious ways. It means that he's given me a second chance to be a mother. If you allow me to, I would like to become a part of your life, become a part of your daily routine. I know this is a lot to understand, but please don't shut me out. I don't know if I could take rejection from you. I just want a chance, a fair shot, Zamaria, I mean, A'miracle. I want a fair shot at being your mother. Can I have that?" She asked, in such a sincere way. This was definitely a lot to process, but there was no way I would let this lady walk out of my life for the second time.

"If I agree with this, we do things on my terms. No more secrets; no matter how bad it is. I want to get everything out in the open, so that we can leave the past in the past, and focus on building our relationship. Is that ok with you?" I asked, barely above a whisper.

"Of course, it is," Zofiaa said, embracing me again.

"One last thing, is it ok if I call you Mom?" I asked, as the tears filled my eyes yet again.

"Aww, this is such a magical moment," Eternity said, covering her mouth.

"Of course, you can. I wouldn't have it any other way, my daughter," Zofiaa said, as I hugged her again. Tabari went and opened another bottle of wine and made a toast. At that moment, I've never felt a love like this before, and I planned to cherish every moment of it. God works in mysterious ways, and he makes no mistakes. I was a lucky baby, blessed, actually. Not only did I have a strong biological mother, but I was also blessed with an even stronger adoptive one…

FOURTEEN

Wade

$\mathcal{I}$’ve been stalking A'miracle's ass, and it's crazy that I was so close to her, and couldn't pull the trigger. I wanted her to suffer, and felt like shooting her would be too damn easy. I watched as she cheerfully walked inside of Pete's Fresh Mart. I knew she was probably going to cook this nigga dinner or something, which only pissed me off more. How could she not be grateful for the things I've done for her? She literally, wouldn't be shit if it wasn't for me. Parking my mother's car a few rows down from A'miracle's, I got out and walked over to her car. You would think she would have upgraded her car, or even changed the locks, since I still had a key. This shit was going to be easier than I thought. I unlocked the car using my fob key, and sat in the backseat. It was already pretty dark out, since time went back and it started getting dark around 3:30. It was 6:15, and I patiently waited for her to return. Around 6:35, I could hear her voice. She was laughing, and it seemed like life had been really good to her. Too bad that was about to end. She ended her call, unlocked the door, and hopped inside. The only problem with that was she didn't check the backseat; truly, most women forget to do this. They just hop in the car and pull off.

"Ok, I got everything I need. Time to head home and get

dinner started," she said, as she placed her phone in the cup holder. I took that as my cue.

"Aht, not home, sweetie. We have plans," I said, sitting up and placing the gun to the back of her head.

"Wade! Oh my God! Please don't!" She begged, which only made my dick hard. It's been a long time since I heard her scream out my name.

"Hey, hey, calm down. Breathe. It's ok, everything is going to be ok," I said, looking through the rearview mirror at her. I took a couple of deep breathes with her to get her to calm down, before giving her instructions.

"Now, I want you to do exactly as I say, A'miracle. Please don't make me kill you here. It really wasn't in my plans. Now, drive!" I spat, hitting her collarbone with the but end of the gun.

"Ahh!" She yelled, as she started the car and drove out of the parking lot. I hopped up front with her and kept the gun planted in her side. I knew she was scared, and she should be.

"Why are you doing this?" She questioned, as we heading down the expressway.

"I didn't tell you to talk, now did I? See, you have to listen," I spat, slapping the shit out of her.

"Now, to answer your question, it's a bunch of reasons why I'm doing this. You're a lying, thot ass, bitch! You a hoe, A'miracle, and a nigga was really trying to wife your ass," I laughed, rubbing my nose. I was anxious to get to my mother's house, since I mistakenly left my drugs on the counter. I was feening and needed my fix to go through with this.

"I really loved you, and you just up and moved on. How? I told you we were in this shit forever, and I meant it, beautiful," I said, rubbing the side of her face. It was wet, and she had been crying nonstop, which didn't bother me at all. Her cellphone vibrated, and a picture of that bitch ass nigga, Tabari, popped up. She looked over at me as if she wanted to answer it and I politely shoved the gun harder in her side, to let her ass know I wasn't fucking around.

"Think about if you want to. I will shoot your ass right here, driving down the 290," I said.

"Get off at the next exit," I yelled, as the nigga called back again. He called a total of four times, before we finally pulled up in front of my mother's house. I got out of the car, then pulled A'miracle out. I looked around to make sure no one saw me as I used my mother's keys to let myself in. The moment we were in the hallway and on the stairs, I pulled A'miracle backward against the wall, and forced my tongue down her throat. She tried to fight me off, but I was too strong for her. She let me kiss her, but she didn't kiss me back, that pissed me off, and she would pay for it soon.

"Kiss of death, sweet cheeks," I said, slapping her ass and forcing her up the stairs. She had gotten thicker from the last time I saw her. I wondered if her pussy was still wet as Niagara Falls? We made it to the second floor and inside my mother's apartment. I guided her to the bedroom where my mother was laying.

"Oh my God!" She screamed, looking at my mother on the floor. It was blood everywhere, but she wasn't dead. I didn't mean to shoot my mother, but then again, I did.

"Get on the bed!" I demanded, as A'miracle slowly followed my directions. Tears were pouring from her eyes, and honestly, I didn't give a fuck. She brought this shit on her own. My mother was a little freaky bitch, since she had a pair of handcuffs in her dresser. I knew since my mother was fucked up, I didn't have to worry about her trying to get away. As far as A'miracle, I knew this lil bitch was going to try me. To prevent me from killing her too soon, I decided to handcuff her ass to the bed.

"Wade, you don't have to do this. Please, just-"

I didn't even let her finish her sentence, before I backhand her ass.

WHAM!

Her head snapped hard to the left, before blood dripped from her lip.

"Wade, please stop. Please, just let me go," A'miracle cried. She looked pitiful to me. I walked away from her and headed to the kitchen. Picking up the bag of white powder, I emptied it on the counter. Using my mother's credit card that was in my pocket, I lined up the drugs just the way I liked it. With the rolled up twenty, I snorted two of the lines quickly, feeling the warm tingly feeling all over. I never meant for shit to get this bad, but it did, and there was no way I could fix it. Images of C-Mack's dead body invaded my thoughts, and I found myself snorting two more lines, four more lines, six more lines, until the bag was empty. I found myself getting higher more days, just to get rid of the thoughts. Going to the small bar my mother had, I grabbed a bottle, popped the top and drunk it. I didn't even know what the fuck it was, but I wanted to get as far away from reality as I could. Once I felt completely relaxed, I headed back to the bedroom where A'miracle was.

"I never meant for things to get this bad, I swear, I didn't. I really loved you, and prayed that we could work things out. People get into it all the time and makeup. Why couldn't we do that? A nigga had real love for you, and only wanted to see you succeed. Yea, I had a problem keeping my hands to myself, but some of that shit was your fault," I spoke, truthfully.

"My fault, Wade? How was it my fault?" A'miracle spat.

"Your smart ass mouth! How else? You never listened to a nigga, and I know what's best for you," I spat, turning the bottle up again.

"Wade, you don't even know what's best for yourself! How the fuck will you know what's best for me? You wanted to know my every move; where I was, who I was with, what times I left places, just because of you-"

"You damn right I did! I'm your nigga, I'm supposed to know this shit. Fuck wrong with you?" I snapped, looking at her ass like she was crazy. Her face was swollen on the side that I slapped her. I was starting to feel sorry for her, but her smart ass mouth took those thoughts away. I didn't wanna hurt her, but she was making the shit so hard.

"You're not my nigga! You're not my man! Men don't act like this, Wade! Men don't put their hands on women, unless it's to make them cum! You hurt me so bad, and expected me to come back to you! I'm not a weak bitch!" A'miracle screamed. Hearing her say that shit only pissed me off more. Walking over to the bed, I strad-dled her ass. I needed to be as close to her as possible to let her know who the fuck was running things. I grabbed her throat and choked her as I spoke.

"I would rather have a weak bitch, than hoe ass bitch! All it took was for one disagreement for you to go hop on the next dick! You better than that; at least, I thought your ass was! You know how stupid you made me look?" I asked, squeezing her neck even harder. Finally letting her go, I watched as she coughed. The bitch was lucky I didn't choke her ass to death.

"I needed you, A'miracle! I needed your ass to ride for me! I needed you to stick by me, no matter what!" I spat, getting up and pacing the floor. My mother started moving and moaning, which pissed me off.

"Ugh!" I spat, irritated. Quickly, I placed my gun on the dresser, and I picked her ass up and propped her against the wall next to it.

"Oh my God! Dominique!" A'miracle squealed, looking at my mother. I was lost as to how they knew each other. My mother's eyes opened a little, then closed. Her skin was pale, and she lost a lot of blood.

"Wade, she needs a hospital or she's going to die. Please, just let us go," A'miracle said.

"Fuck that! She deserves to die! She left us for dead, fuck her!" I yelled, letting my emotions get the best of me. I kicked my mother in her leg, causing her to scream in pain. I was so damn mad at the both of them, and wanted them both dead.

"Who could be so cruel to their mother? How could you think any of this is ok? You better pray and hope Tabari doesn't find you. My man is going to come for you, and kill your ass about me, no doubt about it," A'miracle stated.

"He loves me, all of me! He's a better man then you'll ever be! You're a waste of fucking air! A fucking nobody, who kills people then runs! You didn't think I knew about that, did you? How the fuck are you claiming to be this heavy ass nigga in the streets, and running like a punk ass nigga? You a straight bitch! I don't give a fuck what you do to me! One thing for certain, I won't go down begging! If you're going to kill me, then kill me. But take this fuck you with you, bitch!" A'miracle screamed. My blood was boiling as I looked at her. How could she tell me some shit like this?

"Bitch, fuck you! You wouldn't have shit if it wasn't for me! I made you, bitch!" I screamed, lunching for her. I punched her ass multiple times all over her body. I was livid, and wanted her to feel exactly what I felt. When I finished, blood was everywhere, and she wasn't moving.

"Shit!" I yelled, running to the bathroom to get a towel. I felt like I was having an out-of-body experience that I couldn't control.

"A'miracle, baby, I'm sorry. Wake up, please," I said, as my hands shook. I was trying to wipe the blood off her face, and slapped her a few times. Her face was so swollen, blood was coming out of her nose and mouth, and I knew I fucked up, because she still wasn't moving. I didn't even know how to check and see if she was breathing.

"I'm sorry. I'm so sorry," I said, trying to lift her up.

"A'miracle, please, talk to me, baby. I love you. I always have. I didn't mean any of the shit I said. You got a nigga in his feelings, and-"

CLICK!

I couldn't even finish my sentence since I heard a gun click behind my head. Easing my way off the bed, I stood frozen, losing all my ability to move. I looked over at A'miracle one last time.

"I'm sorry, Mama. I'm sorry I let you down," I said, looking at her. She propped herself up against the dresser, using the little strength she had to hold the gun up. If I wanted to, I could have got it from her, but I didn't.

"A'miracle was right. I'm a waste of fucking air. Put me out of my misery, Ma. I don't belong here," I said, as the tears finally rolled freely.

"Goodbye, son," was the last thing I heard, before the gun went off.

POP! POP! POP!

FIFTEEN

Tabari

"The last time I spoke with her she was leaving the grocery store. How could she not be here?" Eternity stated, as she paced the floor. I had called everybody trying to see where A'miracle was. It wasn't like her not to come home, and just up and disappear. I called her multiple times, and the phone continued to ring. Something was telling me something wasn't right, but I didn't wanna panic. My doorbell rang, and Keahi walked over to open.

"Where is she? Has she called?" Zofiaa said, just as worried as I was.

"No, she hasn't. She won't answer the phone. She always answers for me," I said, pacing the floor. I called Melissa too, to see if she stopped by to see her father, but she said she hasn't seen her. This situation was fishy, and I felt myself getting ready to spazz.

"What about the police?" Eternity stated. Before I had a chance to answer, Zofiaa did.

"They won't help unless she's been missing for at least twenty-four hours. So that would be a waste of time calling them. Did you guys get into it, have an argument?" Zofiaa asked me.

"Nah, what would we argue about? I love that damn girl. Our relationship is solid," I spoke, calling her again.

"Still no answer," I said, tossing my phone on the couch.

"Track her down by her phone," Zofiaa said, making me feel stupid. I totally forgot about that. I looked up her location, and it was odd.

"It says she's in Forest Park. Who lives out there?" I asked, looking over at Eternity. They were best friends, and maybe she knew something I didn't.

"I don't know, and don't look like that. A'miracle loves you. She will never cheat. I know personally," Eternity stated, reassuring me.

"Looks like we going to Forest Park," I said, as we all headed out the door. Keahi drove, while I sat in the passenger seat. Zofiaa followed us and Eternity decided to ride with her.

"Man, I hope this ain't no bullshit," I expressed. I trusted A'miracle, and I prayed she wasn't about to make me look like a damn fool. I loved this girl. I put my life on the line for her, and this would crush me if she's cheating. We got off the expressway and let Siri direct us. Pulling up, I saw her car, and Keahi double park. Jumping out, I ran over to the car, but she wasn't inside. I decided to call her again, but the moment I saw her phone in the cup holder, I knew some shit wasn't right.

"Her phone's in the fucking car!" I yelled, as everyone walked over to me.

"This doesn't make any sense. Who the hell stays here?" I said, looking at the apartment building.

"I know this place. One of my girls stays here. Actually, Dominique stays here. They never talked during the sessions, and I believe they only saw each other once," Zofiaa said, with a blank expression on her face.

"Who the fuck is Dominique?" Eternity questioned.

"She's one of my patients. I don't know if you guys remember the young girl who was killed a while back; in the club. Her name was Dove, I think. That's her mother," Zofiaa spoke, as Eternity started shaking. When she said Dove, it felt like my heart dropped.

"Her?" Eternity asked, holding her phone up with a picture of Dove on the screen.

"Yea, her. What's wrong?" Zofiaa asked.

"Oh God! No," Eternity said.

"What's wrong? I don't understand," Zofiaa stated.

"We gotta get in this building, man," Keahi stated, as he walked over to the door. I watched as he looked at the names before pressing all of the buttons.

"Someone will buzz us in," Keahi stated, pushing the door.

"If not, we breaking in this motherfucker," I spat.

"Dominique is Dove's and Wade mother," Eternity stated, just as we heard gunshots.

POP! POP! POP!

"Oh God, please!" Eternity screamed.

"Move, Keahi! I'm kicking this bitch in!" I screamed. Just as my foot was about to connect with the glass, the door buzzed. Instantly, we all ran inside and up the stairs.

"What door?" I asked.

"Third-floor, door B!" Keahi yelled behind me. I was the first one at the door. With one quick motion, I kicked the door off the fucking hinges and ran inside.

"A'miracle! A'miracle!" I yelled, looking around. I didn't see anyone in the living room and made my way through the house. The faint smell of blood and gun smoke lingered through the air. Pulling out my gun, I walked over to the door that was closed. I motioned for Zofiaa and Eternity to get out of the way. I looked at Keahi and nodded before opening the door.

"Oh God, baby! A'miracle!" I yelled, running over to her. The entire room looked like a blood bath. Wade was dead. His brains were on the wall behind him and floor. A'miracle was slumped over on the bed, with blood all over her face.

"A'miracle! Hold on, baby!" I said, trying to free her from the cuffs.

"Keys... Top drawer," a faint voice said. I looked over at Keahi, who was staring at the woman.

"Oh my God!" Eternity screamed. Zofiaa came inside the room and didn't know what to do. I watched as the tears rolled from her face, and I didn't need tears right now. We needed to save my baby's life.

"Come on, find the keys!" I yelled, as Keahi went to the drawer. Eternity started praying before picking up her phone.

"Don't call the police! We gotta get her to the hospital," I spat.

"Here!" Keahi yelled, tossing the keys my way. My hands shook as I freed A'miracle from the cuffs. As soon as I picked her up, she screamed.

"Aghhh!" She said, finally opening her eyes.

"I got you, baby, I got you. Stay with me," I said, as I walked out of the room.

"Help me get her," Zofiaa said. I watched as Keahi picked up Dominique, and we all made our way back down the stairs. By now, neighbors had come out of their apartments, and I could hear the sirens.

"What do we do?" Zofiaa asked.

"Put them in the cars! Let's go!" I yelled. I slide A'miracle in the backseat and got back there with her. She had a gash on her head, which was bleeding pretty bad. Her eyes were swollen shut and her lip was busted. Her nose looked broken, and I couldn't help but get angry.

"Aghhh! FUCK! FUCK! FUCK!" I screamed, punching the roof of the car.

"Stay with me, Bear! She needs you! We in Forest Park, and Rush Hospital up the street," Keahi said, trying to calm me down. I took my shirt off and applied pressure to her head. Keahi was speeding through traffic, and I looked behind me, and Eternity was right behind us. We ran lights, damn near hit a couple walking across the street, but we made it. Pulling up to the emergency room, I jumped out with A'miracle in my arms. This time, she didn't say anything, and her body felt so heavy in my arms. I ran through the emergency room door, just as Keahi ran to Zofiaa's car to get Dominique.

"Help me! Please!" I yelled, as the security alerted staff. Moments later, nurses ran through the double door to my left.

"Come with us!" The nurse stated, as I ran through the doors with them. We made it to the first bed I saw, and I placed A'miracle on it. Keahi placed Dominique in one of the beds in the hallway.

All the nurses came to our aid as I watched them work on A'miracle.

"This one needs to go to the OR, now!" The doctor said, referring to A'miracle.

"Gunshot wound to the chest needs OR, now!" Another nurse said. They worked quickly on both A'miracle and Dominique, before they rushed them to surgery.

"Please, save her. I can't lose her. I can't lose my baby again," Zofiaa cried, finally breaking down. The security and one of the nurses escorted us back to the waiting area. I couldn't even think straight.

"I was supposed to protect her. I was supposed to save her. I failed," I spoke. The moment Keahi's hand touched my shoulder, I broke down.

"God, please, I'm begging you," Eternity prayed, just as Melissa walked through the doors.

"Where is she? Where is my baby?" Melissa said, looking at us before she broke down too. The only thing we did was cry together. The moment I saw my mother, I instantly thought something was wrong.

"Ma, what's wrong?" I spoke, walking over to her.

"I heard about what happened. Keahi texted me. The stuff is all over the news. I couldn't let you go through this alone, baby," my mother said, just as another nurse came and escorted us to a private room. Once inside, my mother turned on the TV. She was right, it was all over the news, but no names were released but Wade's.

"I let the neighbor come in and watch Tiana. I needed to come here. To be here for you all," my mother spoke.

"Bow your heads, hold hands, and let us pray! We must pray harder than we've ever prayed before," my mother said. We all gathered in a circle, bowed our heads, and let the tears flow freely as my mother prayed. I couldn't lose this girl. I would never forgive myself if I did. It felt like we had been sitting in the room for hours, before a doctor finally came inside. The look on his face told me everything, and I prayed it wasn't true...

"We did all that we can, but-"

Epilogue

Dear Diary,

Rewinding time isn't possible. There's no time doctor or salesman to go too. Sometimes we are blessed with a second chance to do something right that we didn't do right the first time. Sometimes we are blessed to love again but, in my case, I was blessed with a second chance at living. Things aren't perfect but what is? I've learned to stop looking for perfect and live in the moments. Make memories with those you can't forget and those you can't live without. My life will forever be changed but the lesson I learned is a blessing in itself.

I was healing physically, mentally, and emotionally. I've learned that love is a constant source of pleasure and pain. I've already been through my fair share of pain, so I was overdue for the pleasures of real love. It's crazy how time repeats itself. Here my mother was, running from my abusive father and I was slowly following her footsteps. She made the choice of a lifetime to give me up for adoption; risking her life just to save mine. Who would have thought time would work in our favor? Who would have thought that God would cross our paths again? Who would have thought God would give us a second chance? I was heading down the exact road my mother went down, and I almost lost my life too by choosing to love a man more than I love myself...

Wade didn't love me; he loved what I was able to do for him. Love isn't supposed to hurt, and his love did. Love shouldn't be forced and most days it was. I knew our relationship was over long before he tried to kill me, yet I still stayed with him. A part of me felt that if I stayed, proved to be his ride or die chick, that he would eventually change for me. Turn back into the man I fell in love with, but he didn't. I've learned that when people switch up on you, show you their true intentions, believe them the first time. The moment you find yourself in the ring fighting for a relationship by yourself is when you need to be BY YOURSELF!

I was blessed with two mothers; one that carried me for nine months and the other who took care of me for twenty-six years. Now that I was able to have them both in my life at the same time, I've never felt so happy. Who can say they actually have two loving mothers? At first, I thought this transition would be hard for Melissa but her and Zofiaa have become the best of friends. They both are still overprotective of me though, but I love it. On top of that, my father was still living and breathing. He was my miracle, my warrior. The same day, I was fighting for my life, a kidney became available. While I was in recovery he was in surgery. Dominique didn't make it and come to find out she was my father's kidney donor! Crazy right? She was definitely an angel in my eyes, and I prayed God reunited her and Dove.

Melissa said the oddest thing happened, my father woke up first asking about me and when I woke up, I asked about him. The doctors said maybe we were dreaming about one another, which could be true. Tabari said the doctor told him I died twice. From the blunt force trauma to my face and head, it cracked my skull; applying pressure to my brain. I had surgery on my head and neck. I was paralyzed for three months. With therapy, I finally regained feeling in my legs and was able to walk again; guess I really was a miracle...

Tabari, my knight in shining armor. Words can't express how much I love this man. He has been by my side every step of the way. I was in love with the way he loved me. In love with the way, he cared for me. I was in love with the way he accepted me now, accepted my family and welcomed them with open arms. They don't make them like him anymore. He was indeed my everything and I was blessed to have him. I would spend the rest of my life making this man happy if it takes my last breath.

Eternity, my best friend has been my ride or die. She has literally stepped up to handle business for me. She put her wants and needs to the side to make sure I was straight. Since the accident, and partially losing my sight in my right eye,

Eternity has been right there. Tabari actually had a building built for me with his construction company attached to it. The bank finally cut me a real check and I couldn't be happier. Eternity now oversees my business with my assistant. Eternity cracks jokes at times about my glasses, but I know it's all out of love. Once I healed completely then I would return to work. I can't let anything stop me especially since I fought so hard to survive. I got my name changed and added Zamaria as my middle name. Both of my mother's thought that was a great idea. I was covered in love, surrounded by love and most importantly covered in strength. I was a living miracle. I will always be A'miracle always have been and always will be...

THE END

TO MY READERS

Thank you so much for your love and support! Book 13 is complete. I really hope you enjoyed this series just as much as I enjoyed writing it. This story took a lot out of me, just because I'm a survivor of domestic violence. It doesn't matter if it's physical, mental, or emotional, love is never supposed to hurt, or make you cry. If you're in a domestic violence relationship, my prayers go out to you, and I hope you can find the strength to realize you deserve better. If you, or anyone you know, are involved in a domestic violence relationship, the national domestic violence hotline number is listed below. Thank you so much again for your love and support.

   -Xoxo J'diorr

NATIONAL DOMESTIC VIOLENCE HOTLINE: 800-799-7233

CPSIA information can be obtained
at www.ICGtesting.com
Printed in the USA
LVHW111816130319
610529LV00003B/252/P